(07/05)

The Last Llanelli Train

The Last Llanelli Train

Robert Lewis

W F HOWES LTD

This large print edition published in 2007 by
W F Howes Ltd
Unit 4, Rearsby Business Park, Gaddesby Lane,
Rearsby, Leicester LE7 4YH

1   3   5   7   9   10   8   6   4   2

First published in the United Kingdom in 2005
by Serpent's Tail

A CIP catalogue record for this book is available
from the British Library

ISBN 978 1 84632 906 7

Typeset by Palimpsest Book Production Limited,
Grangemouth, Stirlingshire
Printed and bound in Great Britain
by Antony Rowe Ltd, Chippenham, Wilts.

'Et delator es et calumiator, et fraudator es et nego-
tiator, et fellator es et lanista. Miror quare habeas,
Vagerra, numnos.'

'You're an informer and a muck-raker, a fraudster
and a conman, a cocksucker and a bad influence.
All this, Vacerra, and amazingly, you're still broke.'
Martial, *Epigrams*, xi-66, first century AD

'Behind every piece of virtue on this earth there
is a legion of aching hearts and empty pockets.
Somebody has paid. I know.'
Gwyn Thomas, *O Brother Man*, 1936

PART I

ENNUI

CHAPTER 1

The White Hart was over on the other side of Victoria Park, in Bedminster. It was a rough, joyless hovel, the landlord was an idiot, and I didn't like any of the locals. All the places I went to tended to be like that. My needs are not great, and let's not deceive ourselves as to what are needs and what are not. Let's have the nerve to face them for what they are, right? It works out cheaper that way. Usually.

I'd blagged the advance from a new job just in time to make it for opening. In some pubs, especially the older ones, if you can catch them in the cold glare of a bright morning, the dust diffuses the light inside into this soft cloud of opaque whiteness, and it looks like oblivion. Dawn can put that sort of spin on a pub sometimes, even pubs like the Hart. The only regulars I knew by name didn't turn up until six or seven: Declan lived off house painting and fruit machines and Johnny had been in the French Foreign Legion. I don't know what he did with himself these days. Somebody said he knocked off post offices, which wasn't unbelievable.

'How's the peeping Tom business, then?' asked Declan when he saw me.

'All right.' I said. 'Busy day?'

'Not me, no chance. Working in this house up in Clifton, and they may be rich but they don't have a fucking clue, mate. Two and a half hours I did today. Funny how the toffs are supposed to be so smart, innit?'

'Get up to much?'

'Well, I had to see Jason about some stereos.'

I nod.

'Don't want a stereo, d'you?'

No, I don't want a stereo, and if I did it wouldn't be from anyone who was on business terms with Declan.

'How are you, John?' I ask. Johnny hasn't spoken to me yet.

'All right,' he concedes, begrudgingly. I'm reading an article in the paper about Michael Portillo's hair before the football finally comes on and gives us all something to do.

Arsenal beat Derby 2–0. I stare blankly at the screen thinking of other things, chorusing whatever criticism seems to be universally expressed. I don't like football, I suppose, but I don't dislike it either. It has its uses. Conversation turns to future fixtures, about City, about Rovers, about football and sport in general. This night at least is saved from anything as embarrassing as politics.

Someone mentions the Tyson – Bruno fight. 'There's nothing I love to see better than two black bastards kicking the shit out of each other,' says Johnny, to general laughter, and I can hear myself among them; can catch the hollow, humourless ring of my voice, its quiet plea for acceptance.

Then next thing somebody's pulled the blinds all the way down for a lock-in, and I watch them unfurl like little flags, signalling the arrival of my session at what must be by now its twelfth hour. I order a large after-hours brandy and smoke a panatella at the fruit machine. I have a vicious argument with a sixty-year-old man about a professional golfer I've never seen play. I stare blatantly at the young girl in the corner until her boyfriend stares blatantly back. I offer the land-lord a drink. He declines. I buy Declan a lager. Johnny always buys his own.

I listen to Johnny, unusually gregarious, talk openly of the whores of Hamburg and recall with some-thing like pride the nights when legionnaires would gather round to drink Kronenbourg and mastur-bate over hard-core porn. I was thrown so much I had to go and put another tenner in the fruit.

After ten minutes, through means entirely unknown to me, I have scored fifteen pounds. The inevitable catch, of course, is that you can only collect after another win, and I'm busted shortly afterwards. Then, as I'm about to chuck it in, the fruit grants me a continue. In an effort to meet the ten-second deadline I extract the entire contents of my pocket in a single futile fistful. Change goes everywhere but the slot.

I succumb to this incoherent, blithering fury, but it dissipates when my blurred fingers prove unable to pick up the coins, and I watch them struggle, marvelling like an infant, bemused by the strange knowledge that this seemingly sentient flesh was part of my own body. I knew then that the evening's real deadline had obviously been met and, persevering for what felt like an hour, I carried what I could to the bar in scooped hands. The barman took it all in exchange for a final brandy and the gag reflex shook my stomach like a depth charge.

'See you tomorrow, you bastards,' I say, buoyantly, to nobody. Then all that remained was to salute the nearest human figure, turn, rebound off the door frame and slide out into the street. Give it half an hour or so and I could strike another day off the calendar. God knows, it was the only way to tell them apart.

I broke the ascent of Victoria Park with a gasping fag and sat on the low stone wall surrounding the primary school. You can see the heart of the city from there. I still got the odd, fleeting moment of awe, looking across the railway lines at the campanile and the Clifton bridge and the rising rooftops of the hills. Which is sheer foolishness, not least because this city has long made it perfectly clear I am not wanted, although it lets me stay on for unspoken reasons of its own.

It is all I can ask for. I couldn't go back home now any more than I could have stayed there in the first place. It's not far, I know. Maybe it wasn't far enough, but I do not see myself in London or Edinburgh somehow. I've never been a man to do things by halves: a quarter, or maybe a third, is as much as you get. Perhaps it doesn't make much difference, perhaps the conventional wisdom is right: people find their own level, wherever they are. I seemed to have found mine.

Rested, or at least resolved, I stand and stub my fag out on the school wall. There's eight feet of chain-link round there too, of course. They put it up a couple of years ago, after the disappearances, which was too late for some. Somebody finding their level, as conventional wisdom would have it.

On the far side of Windmill Hill the spectral glow of the city's centre finally disappears, leaving me in darkness till Wells Road. Not country darkness: it is still light enough to make out the park's regulars shifting about in the distance. It gets more visitors at night than it ever gets during the day, queers and junkies and people whose problems you couldn't begin to fathom. Whatever they were after the pubs, clubs and contacts had failed them, and now they were here, and still searching. Some idiot has even tried to approach me for a rumble in the bushes once or twice. Me of all people. Oh yes, I have left this place fuming like a feminist at a building site on more than one occasion.

There were more of them around the gates. As I say, I'm not truly homophobic, but I have to stare at them very hard when I walk out, I have to use all the venom and bile I have left to keep them silent and distant as I go, and it is only just enough. Years ago I could have been genuinely threatening.

Another uphill stretch and then it's back to Totterdown, named after the steepness of its streets. So a man in a pub told me once. I had found myself unforeseeably sprawled out against the pavement enough times for this to sound credible, although it was not a practice I confined to Totterdown alone.

Between Wells Road and the Arnos Vale cemetery there's a web of identical red-brick terraces, perched tenaciously on the ridge over Temple Meads, and I had a first-floor flat in a conversion round there that was about a month or two behind in the rent. It had its own front door, though, and when I'd crossed the cracked concrete garden I leant unsteadily against it while I fished around for my keys. Which weren't there.

My frustration ricocheted around the empty streets like a mortar round, leaving me silently shameful in its wake. I awaited, for an instant, the appearance of angry heads at bedroom windows, but the people round here know better than to complain. I swore again, calmer now. I do not have my keys. They are, I presume, somewhere on the floor by the fruit machine in the White Hart. The White Hart is going to be closed. I have a spare set though, just like anybody else. I keep them in the flat. Just like anybody else.

Quietly continuing my obscene mantra I fumbled

instead for a lighter and a fag. I'm out of breath, I notice. I'm out of breath almost all the time now. In my jacket pocket I still have the keys to the office, which is less than twenty minutes away and yeah, OK, I tell myself, all right, heading off as the sound of my footsteps and rasping lungs fills the sleeping street. My office is above the mini-market by the traffic lights on Wells Road, and after the two flights of stairs I can barely wrap the rug from reception round me before collapsing.

I say my office but it is still McKellan's. Luckily the man seemed to live an isolated life, because no executor ever turned up to divvy the spoils. McKellan had taken out a thirty-year lease on the place some time in the early seventies, back when I was younger than I care to remember and had nothing to with anything like this. It was going to expire in the next few years, but I'd been too scared to find out exactly when because there was no way I could afford the place afterwards. I had enough problems paying my own rent, and if it wasn't for Maggie I'd have turned reception into the office and put a bed in the back years ago. This sounded like an especially good idea when I woke up on the carpet. It wasn't even seven when my eyelids peeled apart, my body sore and stiff. I closed my eyes again and hoped for the best but it was no use.

Hangovers these days echo of something which was never there before. In younger days they were the fruits of release, to be cheerfully and roguishly endured, but now they seemed more like the flaring symptoms of some hidden, perpetual disease, and they smelled of defeat. They didn't get any easier either; this one was pretty bad. Usually I suppose I had a few units floating around me at any given time but of late work had been too thin on the ground for the bottle, which I can tell you was very thin indeed. You come back to it cold and it can be a killer.

There isn't much that can be done. I stared blankly out across the carpet at a small section of wall that interested me. I turned gently on to my side, causing minimum disturbance to the inner organs. I stopped thinking, absolutely, for minutes on end. I could have lain there for weeks. I don't know what brought me out of it. Whenever these mornings passed it felt like a miracle.

I stand up, once I've mustered the courage. I feel pretty pleased about that, about standing up. It constitutes a great symbolic action. A man who can stand up is evidently a man who can walk around a bit, who can open doors and drawers and shuffle papers and generally look useful. I'm upright now, but wobbling, and sighing profanities I try the length of the office. Not a problem. I walk back again, and then, confident now, I saunter over to the window and stare at the park for ten minutes or so. It was a quarter past seven, too early for the lone pensioner to make his customary crossing of Windmill Hill. I liked to keep an eye out for him. Every week his step seemed shorter, and his gait more crooked, but you could set your clock by him. Or at least you used to be able to, until yesterday.

Yesterday, at the summit of Windmill Hill, he had collapsed, leaving me to wonder whether I was going to call an ambulance, whether I was really the sort of citizen paramedics found standing in the rain at these events. Then this woman had arrived and started talking silly money and I never got to find out. By the time she had gone he was nowhere in sight, and I was on another entrapment again.

'I don't mind paying over the going rate,' she'd said, without too much prompting, and that pretty much got my attention right there. There is no going rate in this job – we're like plumbers, we charge whatever we think we can get away with, and there's no need to worry about repeat custom because it doesn't exist. Mugs' money, all of it. I wrung a few hundred quid out of her for my 'retainer' and told her I was very busy, a lot on at the moment, that I'd ring her tomorrow, anything to get her out of the office.

She'd blabbed on about her husband and what sort of woman he'd be likely to go for and a few other extraneous details before I could get shot of her. Before I could hear her heels clattering out on the tiles of the hallway. Oh Lord, save us from these fattening housewives with ambitions they picked up in magazines. Still, I am not a rich man, and there is nothing else I can do now. McKellan would turn purple with simmering rage if he were around to see it, but if he were around at all I wouldn't have to do it. With McKellan around the business would still be firmly on the side of law and order and the general good, which is easily done if you're a self-righteous bastard with the right connections.

It looked like Maggie's almost certainly fictional flu was still raging, for which I was grateful. She didn't do an awful lot, and to be fair the size and frequency of her pay reflected this, but she was good for the old self-esteem. In spite of the differences between me and McKellan I am still, if nothing else, an employer. It ruined the pretence somewhat when she caught me hung over to the point of paralysis, although she was always too polite or too apathetic to say much about it.

Apathy was something she had to learn, or relearn, after McKellan went. It's hard to imagine, but I'm sure there was something between them. There can be no other explanation as to why a dour Scots Presbyterian would pay secretarial wages to a widowed cleaner who couldn't type. I don't begrudge them whatever real happiness they had, if any, but life gets harder every year, and if you insist on carrying around obsolete expectations you aren't doing yourself any favours. They weren't that old, not really, but they were old enough to know better. It wasn't jealousy which made me wince to spot a lingering hand. A blind man could have seen it coming, one way or another. She hardly came in at all now, and the cleaning was done every other week.

Slowly I edged myself to my desk. I could have sorted the mail, but backing off from anything truly productive I opted instead to take one of Maggie's women's magazines and sit on the toilet until the café opened. In the cramped, pot-pourri gloom of the toilet I notice my clothes, damp as dishcloths. I knew it hadn't rained last night, so fearing the worst I take a nominal sniff. I have not disgraced myself; it is only sweat. Then I remember, suddenly, as you do. I had dreamt again that night.

I was in the flat and the lights went. I checked all the switches but there was no power anywhere. The more I tried the smaller the flat seemed, until I had to flee blindly out into the street, and that was in darkness too. I shuffled through the terraces with my hand moving along the brickwork for guidance. The whole city was as black as pitch. I stumbled on until there were no more buildings in reach, and farther still, scared to touch even the ground as the sound of my own breathing became unbearably loud. Then, if I've got this right, there was a man with a lantern selling some kind of tiny vegetable from a stall, and he told me to shut up.

So what to do now? What is there to learn from that? Nothing, of course. They tell you nothing you don't already know, dreams, or they tell you nothing at all. Don't ask me how they made a living out of it, those hucksters from Vienna, back in the early days of the shrink business, those supposed masters of the unconscious. Yet, I considered, looking down at the cheap inscrutable smile of Ruby Raven, astrologer to the stars, who was then staring up at me from between my pale, ill-looking thighs, they were only a recent development in an ancient and lucrative business. Doesn't matter whether you're tracing your constellations on our unseen crania or the heavens above, it's not as difficult as it sounds to convince people that the obvious impenetrability of life's grey slate was never anything more than a mysterious curtain destiny had appointed you to draw back, that all will be known, all will be charted, all will be explained. Bollocks. Only dead people get narratives. Life is not an endless fiction. But there is nothing else we will believe.

So, I think to myself, why not leave all these obfuscations about our personal karma behind you, Ruby, dear? The market isn't fussy on the details, and it isn't going anywhere, and never has. Even racing commentators make a steady buck pushing random horses as dead certs. Stick your neck out. Tell me about my cancer, tell me to go to Bournemouth, tell me what colour her eyes will be. But Ruby Raven was probably too worried about the instalments on her conservatory to go for glory.

After about another thirty pages I reached my limit. Then I knew that I had to leave, to go down to the café even if it wasn't open, even if it meant I had to stand there looking destitute in the cold until it did. Anything to create the impression of activity. Thankfully it was already open, or rather it was opening when I got there, which meant I didn't have to spend any longer than necessary exposed to clouds as dark and ominous as a suspended Steinway in a Laurel and Hardy film. We had been due some heavy weather for days now.

Until recently the caff had been run by a retired couple from Yate, but they'd left for the great caravan park in the sky and two Greek brothers had appeared in their place. Instinctively alarmed, I had been monitoring the gradual changes brought about by their tenancy. Kebabs and chilliburgers were now on the menu, a stream of Greek minicab drivers had begun to sail in and out all day, and none of them seemed to pay for a thing, ever, but that was all. Only a bulldozer could make any difference in here. It had been around too long to be changed by much less, and so had its regulars. Not individual regulars, perhaps, but regular types of individual: any kind of personal recognition would be anathema to the essence of the place. Like the Ford Transit crowd, wider versions of Declan that were actually capable of real labour, albeit in bursts of ten minutes or less. Out of everyone they always showed the most vitality, and understandably so: they were bunking off.

The elderly, being too old or lonely to cook for themselves, were also never absent. It was a popular staging post for those close to embarking on the final journey. If they were going to go they were at least going to have a pot of strong tea in them, you could be sure of that. It seems routine is important to those waiting for death. And then there are the lost and the estranged, those who'll turn up anywhere where they can quietly absorb the company of other people. Ordering the food may be all the actual interaction we get, or would want, but nevertheless a kind of social osmosis does occur. The refreshment is purely metaphysical, when you think about it. No one is in here for the quality of the food, believe me.

The babbling Greeks come and go. A row of defunct pinball machines lines one wall, their burnished chrome buried under the dust of decades. The café racers who played them were gone now, but the pinball machines still lingered, like some kind of monument, and they looked older than all of us.

My breakfast arrives and is both tasteless and scolding. Arms folded, I test my patience while it cools. An old man in a corner stuffs yesterday's *Mirror* into his vest. Outside, the rain is yet to fall. The chef starts getting indignant about something and begins beating his chest, while his brother stares pacifically into a big vat of simmering gravy. Only the minicab drivers understand.

I clear my plate, not without effort, and, predictably thirsty, I leave to buy a litre bottle of Coke from the Pakistani mini-mart and an *Express* to read in the office. Having smoked over eighty the night before I buy just ten Benson and Hedges.

Denial wasn't just a river in Egypt, as Bruce was wont to say.

Back in the office I wheeled my swivel chair out to the middle of the room, where I could see the eerie, apocalyptic panorama of Victoria Park in full, and waited. The old man will make his appearance before eleven if he's still alive, and I make a note to check for his arrival every so often. Then everything seemed to take shape again: another day wedged firmly in my swivel chair, laboriously digesting breakfast with gallons of carbonated sugar and a middle-of-the-road newspaper. This is how I seem to pass my days now, in this strange, semi-comfortable form of solitary confinement.

Yet the office was somehow too quiet for my liking, and too empty, a feeling that had become increasingly frequent of late. I didn't know why. When McKellan was dying I'd given some thought to brightening the place up a bit, expelling the fustiness the man seemed to live in, but it takes more than two pot plants to do that. He'd been here for half a lifetime, and his imprint, his austere aroma of National Service and honest police work, was not to be so easily removed. Maggie might be back before the end of the week, I supposed. Then she could fill the office with her idiotic banter and her radio. When she got too much or spent too much time on the phone I could keep her busy with pointless letters, and then sit back and relax in the typewriter's amateurish staccato.

I had thought about buying her a computer but it would be an expensive joke to play.

I was switching on the kettle in the lobby, absently scanning a lead feature on widows who'd fallen in love with their hairdressers in another back copy of *Have A Break* magazine, when I caught that familiar flicker of agonizingly retarded movement on the brow of Windmill Hill. I had failed him, my unwitting ward, me and maybe all the others who'd happened to be standing at any of the hundreds of windows facing his way, but he had survived. Bundled in trilby and mac he was up and out and at it again, for reasons we were not to know, and I wished him all the best. Even on a good day it took him for ever, and the good days were behind us now, a whole winter away.

Funny the way old people dress up all the time, old men especially. This was where McKellan was heading, always out in your best jacket and tie even if you're buying cabbages. Only the jacket and tie have been past their best for some time now; everything has. All those years at work and war thinking it would finally award them some kind of dignity. They were cheated out of that, somewhere along the way. I watched a veil of sour milk rise to the surface of my coffee with a strange indifference.

The park is always ugly, unkempt, full of mongrels and dog shit, dotted with drunks and the burnt-out hulks of stolen cars. Its trees are few, and fewer every year. Only the rubbish of missed collection days grows happily here. Even the children who visit the

18

playground are almost always alone, and when they demolished the lodge last year they found a month-old baby, wrapped in bin bags, about three days too late. The park is all wrong, but some days, in the cold wind of a coming winter, with a sky the colour of iron ore and the sallow daylight swallowed by the gridlocked fumes of a million angry exhausts as it descends, it is the city that seems ugly. On these days it is the city which seems ugly and the park which looks OK.

Out of the files piled on the floor at the foot of my desk I dug out the studio photograph of the husband I'd been given yesterday. It is already half ten and at some point today I must call this woman, Mrs Dixon, and begin work on her case. The man in the photo was around my age, that's to say he was well into his forties, a nervous-looking type who hadn't been able to keep his eyes fixed on the camera, and the photo was all I really needed to see. I didn't have to know anything about him; it may sound unbelievable, but they all took their bite of the apple. You'd think it was a weakness of the gender. Maybe a faithful man is simply one who doesn't go looking for it: lead me not unto temptation, that sort of thing. Well, that's precisely my line of work.

Along with the photo there was a client sheet I'd made her fill in with a contact phone number on it. I'd dialled the number and it had rung twice before I hung up. She was prepared to hand over a lot of money, and she wasn't the sort of customer

I wanted going elsewhere, but come to think of it I could probably leave it later than this. Best to leave it as late in the working day as possible, without a doubt. About four, say. By that time I couldn't reasonably be expected to do anything until tomorrow.

Pushing the prospect out of my mind I reach instinctively for a fag, and after last night's excesses end up retching like a kid behind the bike sheds. I toy with the idea of putting it out, but of all things left undone I should at least be able to finish this, this expensive, pointless cancer stick. By the third or fourth puff I convince myself it's not an unenjoyable experience. I am under no illusions as to the scale of my achievements in this world.

Six cigarettes, half a litre of Coke and two coffees down the line, boredom breaks through the hang-over barrier. I can no longer fester quietly. In an hour or two I could legitimately get away with breaking for lunch, but to my downfall I am my own boss, and these days I can break for lunch, dinner, elevenses or afternoon tea whenever I want. The racing page in the *Express* is all it takes. The bookies is less than twenty minutes away, opposite the Oxford. I spend two short minutes telling myself I shouldn't, just so I can feel less guilty when I do, and then I'm off.

Bookies, you understand, aren't for real gamblers. They tend to phone their bets in, or do it at the track. If they enter a place like Greenways they will generally place their bet and then leave. The punters in Greenways have nothing to gamble, and their winnings, if anything, are the sound of seconds ticking on an invisible clock. Most bets are somewhere between fifty pence and two pounds. I know several people who can spend six hours in Greenways on a tenner, and a few of them were there when I got round to making an appearance, munching a pasty I'd bought from the mini-market on the way down.

'You can't eat your own food in here,' whines Julie, the instant I enter. I ignore her. She whines constantly. I am unsure whether this is a vocal defect or just her personality. No one would sound happy, stranded behind perspex in this place, but even so. You could at least sound indifferent for part of the day.

'Oh, fuck off, Julie,' Colin deems to protest on my behalf, although he cannot know it is me: his eyes haven't left the form sheets since I walked in. Nothing personal, evidently, just a matter of principle. Colin once told me he was a roadie for Def Leppard. I have no idea how true this is but if Colin ever decided to work, and found employment, it would not include heavy lifting. 'Hello, Rodney. How goes it?' he remarks, when he sees me.

They all called me Rodney. I have no idea why. At first I thought they must have misheard me, but then I was sure I'd never told them my name. More probably it was some private joke at my expense. I never rose to the bait, but they kept at it. That was years ago now. The joke is probably long forgotten but the name has stuck. There are harder crosses to bear.

'Fine. How's yourself?' I answer. Julie is still making some vague whimpers of objection in the background, but my pasty is finished. I make a show of putting the empty bag in the bin.

'Can't complain, mate, can't complain,' Colin answers. And so it goes, until I have had the same half-hearted banter with everyone I know.

'Julie, love, make us a cup of tea,' says Chris, corpulent Chris, from the tiny pursed mouth between the pillows of his jowls. 'Go on, Julie,' he pleads, mockingly, while snatching the waistband of his tracksuit bottoms as they again pass the Rubicon of his navel and rapidly descend the sloping underside of his waist. Watching, you might be surprised at the speed of his reflexes, someone that size, but he's had a lifetime of practice. So we are safe from complete exposure although an arse-crack that would put a siteful of builders to shame remains permanently on display.

None of this bothers him, Chris has uninvitedly confided in me on more than one occasion. Chris 'hides' his huge obesity, you see, under the largest Manchester United merchandise he can find, which is then taken out again and enlarged by his mum. Baggy clothes are in fashion these days, he says. This man must be in his mid-thirties.

'Go on, Julie, you know you want to,' Colin helpfully reminds her. Chris and Colin are what would appear to be good friends and are rarely seen apart. They do, as far as I know, nothing at all, and have done it for the few years I have known them. They're here every day for at least five hours. The place is a shrine to their subtle art. They are the only people I know who can make me feel relatively positive about myself – not very positive, but it is still some feat.

'Hang on a minute,' sings Julie, adhering to an unwritten script, with several daily performances. 'I can't go round making tea just when you ask for a cup. I do have work to do here, you know.' Her voice box must be somewhere around her sinuses. It is not a voice that could ever be loved.

Everyone concedes that Julie is a very busy, hard-working manager and that they wouldn't want to bet anywhere else. Then Julie ruffles some papers for a couple of minutes, so we can see how busy she is, and finally takes our orders, apart from Colin's, as he's still staring pointedly at the form sheet with an exaggerated amount of concentration.

'Why didn't she ask Colin?' I say to Chris.

'Colin's in the doghouse.' He laughs. 'Said something about Pete.'

'Oh.' I nod, understanding. Pete was Julie's husband. Sightings were often reported of cavortings with some school or checkout girl, and if circumstances conspired to make fidelity unavoidable he just spent the night down the pub. Chris and Colin liked to raise the subject in the belief they were rubbing Julie up, and they were, but squabbling with Chris and Colin seemed the only aspect of her marital problems she could handle, and I think she was glad of the opportunity to handle it on one level, however trivial.

'Anyway,' I say, changing subject. 'Tips?' Eventually Chris sidles up and, taking a cigarette from me, tells me in hushed tones to put something on Bloody Mary in the ten past twelve Monmouthshire Handicap Chase at Chepstow.

There are those who find this kind of gambling a lot more enjoyable when imbued with an air of conspiracy; it's one of the components of the fantasy. I tend not to indulge them. Not because it's ridiculous, which it is, but because it is already fantastical enough for me. The people in here will never win. How far can you stretch the odds on a two-pound bet? How many permutations can you go through? Yet they still kid themselves, even the cynical, that one day the reliable connection or winning system or long, lucky streak to glory will be theirs. Even if they don't admit it, the whole thing is just a ritual of not having. It cannot be discounted that any bet remains a mathematical possibility, but I was a debt collector for five years and I know what happens when the squeeze is on. When the squeeze is on you get your door kicked in and your furniture taken away. You do not get the results for Ascot.

Aware of all of this I put a tenner on Chris's tip. Then I forced myself into the terraced rows

24

of narrow plastic seats before the monitors. Bloody Mary started at 7–1 but when I laid my bet it was 9–2.

'You forgot your tea,' Julie reminds me, and brings it over. She likes me, Julie, I think. She would. I'm the only regular who doesn't openly abuse her.

Typically, despite the secrecy shrouding Chris's nap, everybody's backed it. She's light enough to get ahead by a length out of the stalls, and for the first bet of the day to come through could only be a good omen, but the horse is too light. As the pack squeezes up around the final bend some brute forces her back to third.

'Should have put it each way, Rodney,' says Colin with some smugness as he goes up to collect his money, along with everyone else. These winnings will all be under two pounds: I know these people. Only an old man remains seated.

'Well,' I say to Chris when he comes back, 'any other tips?'

'Not like that, my son,' he tells me, taking another one of my cigarettes. 'You wasted that one.'

'Nothing?'

'For the rest of the day your guess is as good as mine.'

'Fine,' I say. You couldn't expect too many tips in one day or these would be rich and successful men, and for Colin or Chris to become either would point to something woefully and profoundly wrong with the world. Chepstow was just about

25

near enough for the connections to come through with something, although like everybody else they were wrong more often than they were right.

If you wanted to take the insider's approach there was always the dogs down at Eastville. I'd been there once or twice myself, ten pound admittance with free chicken and chips on the so-called executive balcony, but dog connections are not the same as horse connections. I've never seen a man get beaten shitless in the car park at Chepstow or Cheltenham, for example, although my experience is limited and times may have changed.

At least partially consoled by these observations, I settle back with my stewed plastic tea, safe and secure in my local bookies, and watch the horses show for the next race at Ludlow. Eventually I put twenty quid on number two because I like his name. He turns out to be 10–1, but, I tell myself, you don't have to worry about selection when you're doubling up. As long as you've got enough money to see it through it's guaranteed. If you've got enough money you couldn't lose if you tried, and if you haven't you can lose as much as you want. Scant seconds before the race starts, Colin leans over and, actually taking the trouble to look over his shoulders first, asks me who I put my money on.

'What? After Hours?' he says, weasel eyes wide under the dark mank of his fringe. His perennial bobble hat suggests a bald patch lurking somewhere among those long greasy lanks.

'Yes,' I tell him, a little impatiently.

'Each way?'

'No. On the nose.'

The eyes under the bobble hat bulge.

'Nutter,' he says.

After Hours takes his place last but one, maybe a whole two lengths behind the main crowd. Before I can tear up my slip the jockey has lifted the whip and he's accelerating through the pack. When he breaks he's still gaining, his rider gradually whittling down the distance between himself and the three up in front. Whittling is not enough, and despite coming back from a bad start the horse still finishes a distant fourth. He has been ridden too easily, and the burst was badly timed.

The old bloke has managed to pick some good ones. He's at the counter for some time, as calm as you like, counting and recounting what must be about a dozen twenties before he folds them into his shirt pocket and stumbles back to his seat. Colin and Chris are pointlessly colluding about something in the corner once more. Doubling up again, I smack forty quid on Anastasia in the twelve thirty with no more thought than a dog shitting on a pavement.

The bell sounds and in betting shops all over the country the race commentator begins another spiel. In a windowless cubicle somewhere outside Nottingham a man is spending another day trying to generate constant enthusiasm over midgets riding horses in big circles for hours on end. For all my other problems I don't earn my crust sitting in a cupboard pretending to be ecstatic about races I haven't bet on for the benefit of people like Colin and Chris, and some gratitude is briefly experienced.

Anastasia comes out of the first bend well behind the leaders and nearly falls at the first fence. The horse moves like it's strapped to a milk cart. In the first ten seconds of the race it dawns on me I'll walk out of here seventy quid down. I cannot believe I have succumbed to doubling up. I couldn't tell you how it happened. I hate myself for it. For the next six or seven furlongs the race is not happening, as far as I'm concerned. I have just spent seventy quid with all the maturity and guile of a schoolboy with a stolen wallet. And then I notice that Anastasia has worked up to the leading two, still two lengths ahead, but when Ming the Merciless clips a fence and loses nerve she breaks to the front. Raglan Boy, now second, starts pressing hard. Anastasia's lead shrinks but holds. One glance and I can see I'm back in the race. As long as Raglan Boy hasn't been holding back, Anastasia is clear to the finish, even if there's only a nose in it. I am rigid on the edge of my plastic, pock-marked seat, mouth gormlessly open. I have backed a winning horse. The old man next to me is rapidly slapping his thigh with a rolled and badly beaten copy of the *Sporting Life*, mumbling under his breath. He has backed Raglan Boy.

At the last fence Anastasia tries too late to back

out. A front leg catches the fence and she tumbles, the errant leg ploughing into the ground at an unnatural angle for several yards till her momentum expires and she falls on to her twisted side. Collecting himself after his catapult from the saddle, the jockey rolls to the side of the track and escapes the oncoming pack by less than a second. We see her mouth open but her screams, or neighs, or whatever noise horses make when they're in pain, are drowned out by the pounding of hoofs. That's all we see before the truck-mounted camera rolls on, sticking with Raglan Boy as he crosses the finish line. The old man is bolt upright now, jubilant. Somewhere off-screen a vet is loading a shotgun. The faller needs to be destroyed, says the man from his cubicle, and then we switch to the dogs at Romford.

'And they're off . . .' Again. And again. And again.

'Fuck,' I say, to nobody in particular.

Oh, anyone can make a profit in principle. Just walk away once you're on top and never come back. After all, your horses have to come in some time. It's just that when they do you'd better realize, you'd better remember, or you'll spend the rest of your life tearing up slips. You'll spend the rest of your life losing and you might not ever know why. I studied the form sheets and looked at the tables but it was no good.

Outside, the day is still as dark and grey as it was when I left the office. A cold wind has whipped up from somewhere, fierce enough to roll empty cans over kerbstones, so I don't spend more than a moment watching the traffic crawl down into Temple Gate, deliberating over what to do next.

The warm, boozy fug of the Oxford was less than twenty footsteps away.

CHAPTER 2

Actually, the Oxford is a quiet pub midday, quieter than most, especially at the start of the week. Two ancient old boys sat in a corner silently guarding their Guinnesses while an under-age barman threw double and triple twenties.

'Sorry, mate,' he says, when he sees me, ducking back behind the bar with playground agility.

I have a bottle of Newcastle Brown to start with. If it's bottled they can only fuck it up at the brewery and I do not trust pubs run by teenagers. I ask him whether there's anything to eat and he says the kitchen isn't open yet but he can get Emma to do me a ploughman's. It'll do. By the time I leave this place I know my hangover will be gone. There are two fruits in the Oxford, one of which, I remember, seems to pay out on a regular basis, and my hand dives for change but I stop it before it reaches my pockets. That stuff's all over, for today.

I find a stool out of harm's way and let my eyes drift up to the dusty screen of the television above the bar. The sound is turned way down, so all I can hear at first are the dull thuds of the darts against the cork. The old men, as good as dead, haven't said anything since I entered. It takes a minute for the horse business to lift and then I realize what I'm actually watching.

Richard and Judy were over. A bearded man in a jacket with patches at the elbows gesticulated over a model of small plastic spheres in various colours, molecular substructures or some such. The Open University was beaming its secrets into untold numbers of neglected boxes. A whole world of knowledge, as useless and intangible to me now as cigarette smoke. It was too late for any of that, and judging by my current company I was not alone.

I quietly issue a few words of complaint. The barboy thuds darts into the board regardless. The old men in the corner don't even blink. Time passes. I can see dust settling in the few faint rays of daylight the lined windows let by.

Emma comes through the door behind the bar, drops the plate on the counter and stares icily at her colleague until she catches his attention. But when the thuds stop and he looks across she says nothing, only turns to me and says:

'D'you want vinegar?'

'Why would I want vinegar?'

'We haven't got any Branston's,' she explains, briskly, as if I'd been expecting caviar. Then, after another harsh glance, she disappears back into the bowels of the Oxford. The thudding resumes. The pickle, I sense, is at the heart of a much wider staff issue. God knows what.

I unwrap the knife and fork from their paper serviette and start to chase a pickled onion around the plate. Lab rats would probably protest over a meal of this quality, but it gives me something to do for five minutes. I order another Brown, and after he's served me the barboy leans up against the bar in a landlordly way and asks:

'Meal all right?'

I had to smile. One stale baguette, one lump of processed cheese, a handful of wilting lettuce and a solitary pickled onion.

'Oh yes.'

He nods knowingly, vindicated.

'Excellent,' I lie, superfluously. He nods again and returns to the steady rhythms of his darts. I eat most of the ploughman's and drain my bottle. I think I saw one of the old men move, but I couldn't be sure. I was about to leave, even if it meant going back to the office, when the old punter, the lucky stranger, comes in from the bookies and plonks himself on the neighbouring stool. He orders a Bushmills and a half of Flowers and takes a decent-sized draught from each before turning his attentions to me.

'Good day at the races, my son?' he asks, wiping the froth from the sparse silvery stubble on his upper lip, understandably pleased with himself.

No, it wasn't, I tell him.

'I haven't seen you in there before,' I say. We get

chatting, so I order another bottle and light up a Benson. I offer him one but he doesn't smoke, not any more.

It turns out he was born and bred round here but moved away after his wife died and he's been staying at his daughter's in Essex until now. Now he reckons he's strong enough to come back to the old haunts alone. I can respect that. How couldn't I?

'Gamble often?'

Not often, he says, but he felt like testing his luck. The old bloke had wanted a good omen and he got one.

'So what do you do, then?' he asks.

'I work for a bank,' I lie. I usually do. I don't have time to go into all that, and it's all the same to him anyway. Then he tells me that he used to be a plumber, and how he used to be in the navy after the war, and then he gives me the usual crap about how 'all this used to be fields'. He was a nice old bloke, really. So I shared another with him before I headed up Wells Road.

'What are you going to do with the money?' I asked, as I got off my stool.

'Oh, I don't know. Buy something for my grand-daughter, something like that. Don't need the money, not at my age.' Yes, not too many of his type around here, I think, heading for the door. Maybe they all went off to live with their daughters.

The traffic was as stagnant as it was when I'd left Greenways. The wind was just as relentless, practically pushing me up the hill to my office.

I'd have been grateful for it if it wasn't for my ears burning crimson with the cold by the time I got there.

The place was a tip. A fog of stale tobacco hung in every room, ashtrays overflowed; my own desk was a miniature Pompeii. The remains of my improvised bed were strewn about the floor. Open supermarket magazines lay around the place like cats, revealing adverts for mail-order dinner sets and adjustable armchairs, and it was probably chillier than it was outside. I felt like opening the windows to warm the place up.

I finished the flat Coke, thumbing through a Marks and Spencer's magazine, fantasizing over pictures of fresh food and clean laundry while the heating kicked in. After ten minutes of begrudged gurgling the place got as hot as it was going to get, so I set to work. After half an hour's muddling it began to look vaguely respectable, and then I knocked a densely packed ashtray on to the floor and ruined a good square yard of carpet. I swore aloud, but the spirit wasn't in me. It was too hard to believe I really expected to make much of a difference. I worked limply through a whole string of obscenities and felt like a schoolgirl. Having no idea where the Hoover was I fled to the lobby, so I could hide the devastation behind closed doors. Over in Victoria Park, empty as usual, you could see the mist of a fine rain creeping over the rooftops of Bedminster. It had yet to let loose, but it was coming. I leant against the window frame, wondering what to do.

I still didn't have the keys to my flat. It was possible one of the White Hart crowd had them, and if they had, it was just possible that they might give them back. But it was too early to start propping up the bar at the Hart, even for me. It seemed there was absolutely nothing left to do except ring the woman and get on with the job. So I went to sleep, face down at Maggie's desk.

When I awoke, startled out of my slumber by a dream I couldn't quite remember, landing stiff necked and wide eyed in her chair, it was four. *Have a Break* was open at the centre spread: 'cheap dresses for the barbecue season'. I couldn't remember ever going to a barbecue. Summer seemed like something that had happened once, years ago.

I put the kettle on and lit up. Then my eyelids were fluttering together again like moths, and despite my discoing heartbeat I felt a weariness heavier now than it had been even in the early hours of morning. Getting any decent rest, I knew, was an impossibility, but it had passed the time. Now the phone crouched ominously on the corner of my desk and I could ignore it no longer.

'Hello?'

'Mrs Dixon?'

'Who is this?'

'This is Robin Llywelyn. Is Mrs Dixon there, please?'

'Speaking,' said Mrs Dixon, who sounded more affected over the phone than she did in person, if such as thing were possible. Nothing quite like the wrong side of the river coming on posh.

'Right. Well, as I told you, I'm extremely busy at present, but I worked flat out yesterday so I could finish my current assignment and now I think I can begin on yours. I should tell you initially it's customary in these cases to begin with a period of surveillance first. I'll get a better idea of his habits, and who knows, there may be more to him than you think.' I told her about the need for basic preparative work, the importance of starting without any assumptions and working from there, all the usual preamble. Nothing too far removed from the typical tutting of a cowboy builder. Mugs' money, as I've said.

'It'll be a complete waste of time,' she said. 'I want you to start work on the entrapment straight away. He isn't seeing anybody else. I know.'

I still had the photo of her husband out on the desk. He had this awkward slipping smile that to my mind seemed to show a little despair around the edges. His wife was right, of course – surveillance was point-less and he probably couldn't bring himself to kiss the receptionist at Christmas, but I wasn't going to miss the opportunity of claiming a few easy days.

'Well, I understand you feel fairly confident about that, but we have to know for sure. If he is already committing adultery you'll have a better case in court. It would also be cheaper and quicker. If he isn't, I'll have a better idea of how to proceed. At this stage, we have to give him the benefit of the doubt.' Benefit, that was a good one. Normal people would have laughed.

'Very well,' she said. 'As long as you can start tomorrow.'

'Fine. Where do I find him?'

'Sorry?'

'Where can I find your husband?'

She wasn't too sure. They had been married umpteen years, they lived together, but she couldn't say.

'He moves around a lot because of his job.'

'I see. Any ideas?'

'Wait a minute, please,' she commanded, and I waited for about ten minutes while I heard her debating the question with another man in the background. Perhaps, I thought, she's having it off with one of his work colleagues. How much he hoped to get out of it I don't know.

'There's already another man on the scene, then,' I said when she came back to the phone, and wondered what it took to make a woman like her blush. I never did. She ignored me.

'He'll be at a place called Caxton House tomorrow. Do you know it?'

I did. It was a squat, nondescript office block by the temporary flyover near St Mary Redcliffe's.

'He'll be driving a black Honda Civic,' she went on. I fished a Biro out from the debris of my desk and wrote the licence number down on a fag packet, which I lost immediately. 'But it doesn't matter. You'll be wasting your time.'

'We'll see,' I said. Then the line went silent. She could sense something coming, I suppose. It was obvious enough. I told her I needed a car and that I was going to get the rental company to bill her. She nearly hit the roof.

It was understandable. Any professional is going to have his own motor, but they slapped a ban on me and I sold it. It didn't make any sense keeping the bloody thing. Suffice to say, I blew all the money, and now I can't see how I'll ever be able to afford another one.

Losing my licence, well, that was it for me. The pointlessness of it all became pretty obvious after that. Work petered out quickly anyway once McKellan was no longer around, but you can't really do this without a car. My clientele and what little reputation I had been allowed to establish disappeared. I don't think there's any way of building them back up, not with things as they are.

The ban was a little gesture from the boys at the station to let me know how I stood. Bruce had always been my only real point of contact with the force, and after Bruce, when they found out I'd made a statement for the internal investigation, things turned cold. My policeman friends and I didn't see much of each other after that, I don't mind admitting.

A few years ago now I'd gone down to the Beefeater on the A38 for the annual do. I don't really know why; it had always been for officers only, even when I was in their good books, and they hadn't asked me out anywhere since I'd grassed. In the immediate aftermath, when I was fighting the awkward realization that I had pushed things too far, I told myself there was no way I could have known. But I did, and it was obvious. In truth I probably went just so I could show a little defiance. For all you can say about them, they respect that. Maybe I even thought I could sort things out.

I turned up late, after the meal, and stayed for the last hour and a half. Four or five pints went down. Knight and Gilboursen talked about football or the weather for a few minutes, nobody else spoke to me. There were a few stares and glares, but that was all. Mostly I sat alone at my own abandoned table among the entrails of exploded party streamers and the ruins of a half-eaten gateau. If I'd gone and stood at the bar there would have been violence.

The night wound up and people drifted outside. Here in the car park, I thought, I will surely get my just desserts. Nothing happened. People weaved back to their cars and drove off, leaving me to wonder whether I had got them all wrong, and then, when I reached the roundabout by the electricity depot, a lad on a motorbike was there to stop me.

'Good evening, Mr Lou-Ellen,' he said, and then he booked me; five years off and a six-hundred-quid fine. That's how things are. That's how it is with me and the Avon Constabulary, and the regional crime squad too, which makes my job difficult, wheels or no. Even Knight and Gilboursen blanked me on the street after that, though they knew it was coming.

But I didn't tell Mrs Dixon any of this.

'Fine,' she said, at last, and left me with the gentle, empty sound of the dialling tone. Fine indeed. I lit another Benson and puffed my way down to the bus stop to catch the car rental people before they locked up and went home.

I'm the only person at the shelter, standing at the roadside like an old man at his garden gate, watching the world go by. Eventually some young doler saunters up in army trousers and what's left of a woolly jumper to share the hiss of his Walkman with me while we watch the sun set over the city. The temperature drops farther still, and not for the first time I think of my coat and wish I hadn't left it in the flat.

I board the first bus that arrives, not bothering to read the destination board, glad to get out of the cold. An old black woman opposite me rocks inanely back and forth, smiling to herself, and on the back seat a tubby anorak in white trainers forages in a Forbidden Planet bag. His cold, piglet eyes met mine with a glance of self-pitying indifference. He wears the same type of glasses as me, I notice. There was a silent and worrying fraternity on that bus, speeding the wrong way into the rush hour. With our faces pressed to the misted windows we watched the frozen torrent of homecoming traffic in the other lanes, a tableau of normal life past which we sailed, four spectres in a ghost ship.

We stopped at Temple Gate and I got out. It was as close as the bus would take me. The garage was probably twenty minutes away, and I set off at a smart pace. I will have to walk the length of Old Market Street, I thought, not without some trepidation; that two hundred yards or so where the city ekes out its skin trade.

It's not hard to spot. Under-dressed women on precarious heels perch in its doorways, pale legs stretched to full shivering length as they lean sucking on their cigarettes. Neon signs advertise books, magazines and videos. The massages on offer here are the real deal, not some pseudo-orthodox New Age monkey business but the oldest form of relief mankind has known. It runs between the newspaper buildings and the police headquarters.

Not all the women are attractive, not by any means, nor what you'd call highly skilled, yet they make their money. Trade is brisk and always has been. What else is there, when another solitary week or month or year goes by and your libido will settle for nothing less than the inglorious conquest of a new pair of thighs? I would know.

We all went, Bruce and me and the rest of them. Being policemen, they made sure they got a discount, and once or twice I had pretended to be one too. Nothing substantial, not a serious shakedown, just a token gesture. Sometimes we

42

went in groups, drunk and laughing. Other times we fucked furtively, alone. If you're a serious officer, Bruce said, then your lifestyle doesn't give you the chance for anything more. I think if you're a serious officer maybe you're probably incapable of anything else anyway, and I was no different. It was reassuring, if not life affirming, to know that for fifty quid an hour there were rooms on Old Market Street where love was something you could put your arms around and beauty was a light switch away.

I hadn't been back there for years, not since they had the internal investigation on Bruce, anyway, not like that. I scuttled past the taffeta doorways and boarded-up windows as quickly as was inconspicuously possible. A sudden realization: if Dixon isn't already having an affair, as is likely, I will, as usual, be back here again. The possibility doesn't thrill me.

Outside the Citi-Centa Sauna I saw the old man who'd got lucky in the bookies earlier that afternoon. It was definitely him. He almost knocked a tottering peroxide blonde in a short white dress out of her doorway as he made his hurried return back to the anonymous street. Yeah, I thought, that makes more sense. He hadn't fitted in at all.

I don't see the garage till I've practically walked into it. It's changed. On the roof foot-high letters spell 'Choice Autos'; before it was known only as 'the garage'. The forecourt has been recently swept and is free of loiterers. The barking of vicious dogs did not herald my arrival. Contrary to what you might think, this does not bode well.

I'd never seen the man behind the counter before in my life. His pressed brown overalls were far too neat for anyone that I remembered working there. 'Where's Slater?' I wanted to ask, but thought better of it.

Slater was an ex-con who would rent me cars without asking to see the licence that I'd lost. We got on well, considering. He knew that the police hated me and that was a good start; I knew half the stuff on his forecourt was stolen, and that sealed the deal. The garage was staffed wholly by recidivists at one point. Now Slater was nowhere in sight, and the place looked legitimate. I dropped a few names as subtly as I could, but the man behind the counter was as straight as his surgically symmetrical moustache.

'I just work for Mr Dinsdale,' he said, hands draped pacifistically at his sides. Maybe they got themselves busted after all: I'd always suspected they'd been up to more than selling stolen cars. 'Do you want to see what we've got?'

The red-and-yellow bunting rasped noisily in the wind above a half-empty yard. A G-reg Sierra rusting in the far corner looked temptingly cheap, but the husband was executive material and the wife acted like money. It'd be an obvious outsider in their neighbourhood. The blue Rover 400 was upmarket enough, and as long as we stayed off the motorways I'd keep up OK. I gave the guy the nod and he took me inside for the paperwork.

'I'll be needing your driver's licence and proof of signature,' he said, handing me a few forms to fill in.

'The other guy didn't.'

'Standard procedure here now, I'm afraid, and everywhere else.'

Before I began to look too desperate I handed over my credit card and a frayed bit of green-and-pink paper that had been invalid for over three years. 'Rightio,' he said, and went off into the back office.

I waited and worried. If he checked the driver's number with the DVLA back in Swansea the whole job was a non-starter. If the guy was especially conscientious he might inform the police, and there'd be a shitstorm. It wouldn't be like them to miss the opportunity.

'Finished?' he asked, on his return. I handed him the completed forms.

'Everything all right?' I asked.

'Oh yeah,' he lied, unknowingly, I have no doubt. 'That's it.'

You lazy sod. I smiled to myself. I could have kissed him. Then he told me the car was forty quid a day with a cash deposit, an expense I didn't have to suffer back in the days when the place was as bent as a nine-bob note, so I ended up paying full whack and it nearly crippled me. I couldn't go creeping back to Mrs Dixon this soon without looking like a complete amateur, and my overdraft was already at full stretch. Leave it till tomorrow, I thought, and with highly honed skill I eased another worry into the shadowy recesses of my mind, a man on a desert island trying not to think of the sea.

It was good to be in a car again. As soon as Dinsdale's lackey disappeared I slammed shut the driver's door and the familiar luxury of it all came back to me. A car is like a womb: small, warm, snug. And they're both extremely comfortable forms of transportation. I turned the heaters on full blast and tuned the radio in. The engine turned over perfectly, which admittedly would probably never have happened in the days before Mr Dinsdale.

The rush-hour traffic was still set in full frigid swing. I edged in with absolutely no idea where to go, carried on its crawling ebb. I had forgotten about the pleasures of driving, the security and empowerment combined. It made the city feel a lot less daunting. At the lights by the church the traffic clogged again and, looking around, I felt a certain kind of brotherhood with the other doleful, pasty-faced drivers, alone in their cars, that I hadn't felt with anyone for a long time.

If I'd let myself drift I could have ended up anywhere. I'd have been perfectly happy to do it too, to just cut out for a mindless hour or four and see where I ended up, even in the five o'clock gridlock, but there was less than a gallon in the tank and I couldn't stop thinking about my keys.

I still took the long way back to Bedminster. Through studenty Cotham, with its launderettes and trendy pubs, across into the gracious colonnades of Clifton, down the bright lights of Park Street and into the wide open space of St Augustine's Parade, then right into Hotwells and right once more, over to the fringes of the city where the fields begin, then sharply double-backing over Brunel Way to the giant old warehouses that line the Avon and the floating harbour, before swinging back into Bedminster through Ashton Gate and the stadium. That just about kills off the novelty for me. I laid the car to rest in the Asda car park and it was seven on the dot when I got into the White Hart again. Keep this up, I thought, and you're in danger of becoming punctual.

I started on the lagers. One or two shouldn't hurt. The place had yet to fill up, and I wasn't going to wait outside like a bouncer. Johnny was already there, and from the state of him he hadn't stopped since I'd staggered out last night. In the time since he'd attracted a small peer group, and they'd formed their own noisy no-go zone at the end of the bar. I'd seen them in here with him before. I think one or two used to be paratroopers, the others were just local characters.

There was a whole network of nutcases in Bedminster, working on some secret psycho wavelength that signalled like a flare gun whenever a spree was on. Somehow they just knew, like dogs before an earthquake, sauntering in, one after the other, for as much drunken violence and violent drinking as they could manage before they drank or clubbed each other unconscious, and when they finally collapsed they went as one, leaving an entire pub to breathe a sigh of relief. It was like watching a felled redwood hit the forest floor.

Regrettably, such an event looked far off. I steered a wide course to the other end of the pub and took a deep dive into a pint of Kronenbourg, thirsty after the hot, stale air of the car, my gratification somewhat marred by the recollection of Johnny's revelation that this is the drink of choice for communal masturbation evenings in the French Foreign Legion. But I got over it. The landlord wasn't much help either.

'Lost your keys, have you?'

'Yes.'

'Nah, I haven't seen 'em,' he said, pulling a Wadworth's for somebody. 'Silly twat,' he added, sympathetically.

'I might have dropped them under the fruit machine,' I offered.

'Nah, I clean that bit of the floor myself every night. Make a few bob that way, if you know what I mean. Understand?' he said solemnly, tapping the side of his nose.

'Ah,' I say. 'Do you know if Declan's coming in tonight?'

'It's not the sort of thing I'd put in my fucking diary, mate.'

'Ah,' I said again, for there was nothing else to be said, and turned my attentions to my glass.

A slow panic mounts. I don't have enough money to pay a locksmith and without my keys I am doomed to another night's sleep in the office, which is no night's sleep at all. What if Declan doesn't show? The only other person I could ask would be Johnny. Scared of making eye contact, I turn my back and hold my pint up to observe his reflection.

He was still in the grips of a real session, exchanging jovial and light-hearted head-butts with friends, and showering half-chewed peanuts on to the bar when he laughed. From the substantial deposits on his clothes and beard he had been finding the night as amusing as his appetite for nuts. But it takes the edge off him, to be honest, his inability to keep his nuts down, and I muster up a little courage.

Shuffling to within earshot of his small Carlsberg commando, I wait for an appropriate moment, for all glasses to be raised, which doesn't take all that long because Johnny and his friends drink a lot more than they talk.

'Sorry, Johnny, but I lost my keys in here the other night and I'm locked out of my flat. I don't suppose you've seen any keys around here, have you?' I say all this to my shoes, to minimize the actual level of contact, but when there's no response curiosity gets the better of me and I have to look up.

Johnny's expression was that which any hard man from fifteen and up has down pat. Johnny needed no imagination to be threatening, which was just as well, as far as Johnny was concerned. Despite the hackneyed theatricals, the food-stained beard and missing teeth, his personal history alone was sufficient. And for those unaware of the seven years in the French Foreign Legion, and those afterwards, his physical profile surely said enough. Johnny was as visibly dangerous as a sea snake in a goldfish bowl. Although I have seen unwitting strangers get a pasting purely because, I suspect, they thought any grown man who acted like that was trying to make some kind of joke.

His friends finish drinking but say nothing. A silence descends which I am long familiar with and it means only trouble. I should have known better than to bother them when they were like this.

'Don't interrupt me,' he says. This is how it begins; I have seen it happen a thousand times before. If no aggravation has been given then some will be imagined. Outdoors they often needed no pretext at all.

'I'm sorry, I didn't mean to interrupt you,' I say, as calmly and sincerely as I can.

'You didn't mean to interrupt me?' says Johnny, missing a beat but recovering nicely. 'Then why'd you fucking do it? Are you some kind of nutter or something?'

'No,' I say, too scared to have to stifle a laugh. 'Sorry, Johnny. I was just making excuses. I interrupted you and I was wrong. I'm very sorry. Please accept my apologies.'

'Yeah?' says Johnny, defiant but obviously confused. There can be no clash of personalities if one side disowns his.

'Well then. I haven't seen your fucking keys,' he answers, finally, and with a detectable air of disappointment.

Mercifully the landlord had a copy of the day's *Evening Post* and I was able to shelter in the safety of its cheap printed pages until the fear and embarrassment subsided. I might as well wait for Declan to arrive. If he hadn't got them, well, I could easily get Johnny to put me in hospital for the night.

Not a lot happened to the city yesterday, according to the *Post*, but then nothing ever does. This is the point of the regional press, I'm sure. Not even the tabloids can offer such a comforting level of banality. Only the provincial papers can maintain that all interesting things happen only to people under the age of sixteen or over the age of sixty-five. Newsworthiness is not the point. Behind every school squash champion, behind the retirement of every lifelong lollipop lady, lay an unspoken aphorism. Nothing you could call halfway profound, but more meaningful than anything extractable from the raw events of your own life. If you read enough of these articles each one started to seem like some kind of fable.

I'm making good headway through a second pint of Kronenbourg and flirting with the idea of chicken and chips when Declan makes his entrance. This is no overstatement: new boots, pressed chinos and a designer shirt, all under a long black leather jacket. A little bit more gold than usual, too, and, more strikingly, a woman in tow. An attractive woman, I should specify. That said, she looks like the sort who work on Old Market Street, but then maybe she does. It doesn't make any difference to me. In any case, money had come in.

Befitting the occasion, Declan did the rounds; he shook hands, exchanged jokes, swapped gossip, bagged jobs and generally tried to look like a bit of a player. He did quite a credible job, actually. I sat back and wondered whether he was going to bother approaching me. He did in the end, which saved additional embarrassment.

'Fine, Declan, thank you. Listen, you haven't seen any keys about the place, have you?'

Declan looked blankly on.

'I lost my keys in here last night,' I explained. 'Seen them?'

'Lost your keys, have you?'

'Yes.'

'Wanker.' He smiled. 'Are you locked out?'

'As it happens, yes.'

'Fucking wanker,' he says, happy to further qualify my character now that he's in full possession of the facts. I would have gone back to the paper but for an unexpected moment of intuition: Declan wouldn't be able to resist flashing his cash in front of the woman.

'Listen, Declan, you couldn't lend me some money until tomorrow, could you? My wallet's in the flat.'

My wallet was actually in my trousers, and it had very little money in it.

'There you go, mate,' he said, reaching almost instantly for his back pocket. The flinch was barely noticeable. 'There's a hundred, just in case, and give it me back tomorrow or I'll break your fucking neck.'

Every bit the ten-bob millionaire, I accepted it with grace and offered to buy him a drink, but he refused, and left. And quickly, too, before anyone else could ask him for money. It would be fair to say I was taken aback. Fifty, I would have thought, tops. The woman must have been important to him. Love, perhaps, or something like it. I drank thoughtfully, considering the options a hundred quid afforded. Even without consideration it was clear that the night, previously a plethora of problems, already had the foundations of potential. Determined at least not to spend it in the White Hart, I left. After the people-packed warmth of the pub the street seemed as cold and dead as ever. Chip papers rolled like tumbleweed across the tarmac. I gingerly fingered my windfall and came to a decision.

Tonight I was sleeping in a Clifton hotel. I was going to buck a losing trend and get out of Bedminster, just for one night. The more I thought about it the more necessary it became. Room service, a proper meal in the hotel restaurant, a few pints in local pubs, and a resident's bar that was open all night. That sort of thing is practically a holiday for me. It was needed just to restore equilibrium, and the alternative wasn't worth thinking about.

There were a few Adidas youths gathered round the Rover when I found it, but as soon as they saw me they scuttled off like mice without a cross word spoken. It would be somebody else's car found burning under a flyover that night. This time of evening the traffic was pretty light all the way up, and I was in Clifton in fifteen minutes. I had changed worlds in a quarter of an hour.

There was a hotel I'd always liked the look of up on Sion Hill, backing on to the gorge. A wide, sweeping Georgian terrace job with a blue canopy over its big glass doors and a lot of brass. The whitewash had started to fade, and the masonry crumble, but it still looked like a posh hotel. I'd never been in there before, nor had reason to.

I parked the Rover in a spare slot on the street outside. It was all parking meters but they were free after six. I made a quick dash for it, with the wind colder and fiercer again up there on Sion Hill, and by the time I breathed out again the heavy double doors had shut silently and securely behind me. I could hear the hum of the air conditioning, giving off a blast of pure heat that felt as luxurious as cashmere, and I was almost overcome.

'You pay in advance,' said the boy in reception, as I finished signing somebody else's name and address in the book.

'I know,' I lied, and handed him the cash, which he reluctantly took. If there was a pair of tongs there he would have used them. I half expected him to ask for a deposit for the room, or personal references. It was a good job he hadn't seen the car I was driving.

'I see we're travelling light, sir,' he said, as he slid the key across the counter top. His shirt collar looked about three sizes too big for his neck. 'No luggage? No coat?'

'Fuck off,' I told him, unreasonably but quietly, and went up to my room before I made a bigger idiot out of myself. There was a time when that didn't happen, that sort of thing, and I still had trouble accepting it. Their jibes may be puerile, or petty, or so subtle and fleeting you had to work hard to hear them, but when the scrawny seventeen-year-olds of the world can abuse you with impunity, well, there are fewer signs of a fallen man so sure. This is a fact.

A quick inspection of the room laid my curiosity to rest. There was nothing in here to differentiate it from any other two-star hotel anywhere in the country, right down to the sachets of coffee by the cordless kettle to the little white soap in the bathroom to the Gideon's Bible in the bedside drawer. It was all that was expected, and it felt clean enough.

There were some fellow suits in the bar down-stairs, drinking on their own. A young and out-of-place French family bickered around a far table, much to our unexpressed annoyance. The face of their small child reddened with a fast-approaching tantrum. Take the child out before it starts to cry, I silently urged them, get the child out. Every other suit there had to be thinking the same thing. There was a time when families like that wouldn't dare enter pubs or bars.

The barman called me sir and managed to sound like he meant it. By the time my Bass was served the first faint tremors of kiddy trouble were already coming, and the father grabbed it and ran for the door like a suicide soldier with a satchel charge. He made it to the lobby by the time the explosion of infantile misery sounded, and we listened to it echo around the bar. It is not something I will ever hear from his perspective. The father, I mean. Too much has passed for that, too much slipped and slung away. I cannot deny I didn't have my chance, but it came too soon, too soon by a lifetime.

That was all you could hear, the kid, and the humble sound of glass against cardboard, when one of a handful of lone, suited men put their pint down on their beer mats. They were sounds that spoke quietly of lost and simple things.

I had another Bass, and the barman still called me sir, and then I left. There was no solace here. It was a room full of people too like myself; depressing, and dull as hell. The number of times

I'd been drinking in Clifton could be counted on the fingers of one hand, and there must be sights to be seen – this was supposed to be the nice part of town – so I went out to see them. I braced the double doors and ventured forth, hobbling over uneven but charismatic cobblestones with the collar of my jacket turned up against the wind and my hands deep in my pockets, walking into the face of the rain, trying to find a decent enough looking pub in a minefield of wine bars and Thai restaurants. I knew I'd wind up back at the hotel bar eventually, but I wanted to take a stab at it.

It didn't take me too long. Never does. Between an upmarket Mexican burger house and a shop that sold Japanese sofas there was a small, square pub cut from Bath stone called the Admiral.

CHAPTER 3

The Admiral expanded away from its modest street-front façade like a concertina, the bar running through a long series of small, separate rooms. I headed straight for the back, just to get a feel for the place, and it took some time.

It was not my standard boozer, but then this was Clifton. They say that if you've got it, flaunt it, but it takes a bit of money to be discreet. There was no karaoke here, no stereo sound system, no wide-screen TV, no nutter at the bar oozing violence. The absence of money has always been more conspicuous than its possession.

The crowd was rugby shirt casual or office-fresh pinstripe. The former camp was twentysomething territory and the latter belonged to somewhere around the high fifties mark. Two opposing sides of the parental divide, men yet to face responsibilities and those who were finishing with them. These were real suits, not like the case-crumpled suits of the hotel. Law or finance mostly, I supposed.

There were some women dotted around the place, jolly hockey-sticks types who spurned sherry and dug drinking with the boys. All well dressed and good looking, to be fair. My Mrs Dixon would give her right arm to get in with that lot. They'd spot her a mile off.

First impressions were neutral but you'd suspect a pub this busy would have something going for it. If I had been in a different part of town I might have guessed it was barmaids-in-basques night, but when I finally got to the bar and saw all the hand pumps I realized I was in one of those real-ale pubs. I went for the old Smiles Best, and got rid of the first one so fast it could have been a conjuring trick. And I wasn't even trying.

By the third I was feeling pretty rosy. Why not? The pub was full of rosy people, after all. It put a little dignity into it, I suppose, pretending you could be a connoisseur of something as perfunctory as getting shitfaced, and this was the place for that. Everyone was at it, and I felt for once like I was somehow strangely qualified. Then I heard some barrister type near me chatting to his friends about speed cameras, something about putting nail varnish on the licence plate to dazzle the flash, which I'd heard a hundred times before.

'No,' I said, firmly, and three grey-haired, clean-shaven faces turned apprehensively to face the only lone drinker in the pub tonight. 'I'm sorry. That's bollocks.'

'Really?' said the one who'd been talking, indifferently.

'Yeah. The flash doesn't tend to cause that much trouble in the first place, because of the distance, and image enhancement will sort out that sort of problem. Basically, if they don't like your car, they're going to have you. If they see a picture of a Fiesta with blurred plates they might leave it, but not a Merc. Or a Beamer, or a Jag; sports cars are all out, obviously, and even the big Japanese saloons might cause offence. If it's any consolation, though, a lot of those cameras aren't on anyway. Run out of film.'

I hadn't made a fool of myself, I don't think. We were, perhaps, on the brink of conversation.

'Well, it was just something a magistrate told me,' he said.

'In the police or something, were you?' said another, with faint disdain.

'No,' I said, 'but I used to have dealings with them.'

'Really?' they said. They were all interested now. I hadn't intended to sound enigmatic.

'Yes.'

'Doing what?' they wanted to know. So I told them, this once, seeing it was not my usual part of town. They laughed and said they thought it was interesting, very interesting. Oh yes, it's very interesting, I told them, a lone man talking to a group of successful strangers, acutely aware he is wearing a cheap and unpressed suit. Then they laughed again and asked whether it was true and I nodded and they asked me what is it you do exactly, if you do that for a living.

Exposed, I scanned their expectant and educated faces for signs of a genuine curiosity, for the nagging knowledge of the roads not taken and the life left outside. Anything to indicate the audience were the captive and not the captors. All I saw was the wry amusement of those who were comfortably settled, and content with their decision to be so.

'Well?'

'You do pretty much whatever people tell you to do,' I replied, and downed my drink. They waited for the punch line but I knew I was the joke, and I wasn't going to let them laugh again. 'Cheerio.'

None of them said anything to me as I shouldered my way to the front of the pub. I realized I wasn't really angry with any of them before I reached the door. They were probably being perfectly pleasant. I didn't know; I wasn't used to the company.

The job is not what I expected it to be. At the back of my mind I had the foolish misconceptions anyone else might have had, having seen the same sort of films and read the same sort of books. The truth was slightly different, and in a short space of time it became an embarrassing occupation to admit to when mixing with decent people. I shouldn't have been surprised; it has been that way with me for a long time. There was a line I crossed somewhere, without knowing it, and then I suppose the wind just changed and I stayed that way.

At the front of the pub, out of sight, I necked a quick whisky, and then I was bracing myself for the elements with no idea of where to go. I knew I wasn't going back to the dire confines of the hotel bar, not yet, anyway, so I stepped into the doorway of the futon shop and lit up, trying to think of somewhere before I started to shiver.

I needed food. Experience told me that ballast was essential if I was to continue, and I had no intention of stopping. The booze was reaching critical mass and some solid matter was imperative to halt the tide. The more I thought about it, the more I had to eat. Suddenly I realized I was ravenously hungry, and the smell of every passing restaurant became an assault on the senses. There was a curry house at the corner of the street and I stumbled in like a man who'd been pulled on a rope.

It was completely empty. Indian food was obviously no longer fashionable among the local elite. It probably stopped being fashionable when Mountbatten left, which was fine by me. A man of my appetites needs undivided attention. Everyone else was at some five-starred Egon Ronay ego-gratification parlour, I presume.

'Table for one?' Some waiters or waitresses ask that question with an enforced and insincere sound of cheerfulness; in here it came with the usual hint of shame.

'Yes, please,' I said, unabashed. 'And a lager with the menu.'

You get some funny beers in Indians, Kingfisher and Cobra and all that stuff. In here Lal Toofan was the house lager – Lal Toofan, named after the red dust storms that whirl through the arid plains of Rajasthan. That's what the label said. It also said it was brewed in Trowbridge, probably by men with names like Colin and Nigel and Baz. Wherever it was made, and whoever was responsible, I don't think there could be much call for it in Rajasthan, even if it is brewed with fucking basmati rice. Something to do, I believe, with the Hindu idea that the consumption of alcohol is incompatible with spiritual growth. Such is the power of religious faith.

When the menu arrives I order another bottle. I already know what I want but it would waste drinking time to go straight for the kill, and I'll need a buffer zone of booze before the spice hits. The waiter returns with his notepad and a third unrequested Lal Toofan: a man of his experience knows when he can pump up the bar bill.

I order onion bhajees for starters and a chicken vindaloo with plain old boiled rice for the main course. I have been in these places enough times to have had everything on the menu twice, and I know what I like.

'Do I get any free poppadoms?' I ask, sounding louder than I'd meant to.

'Of course,' says the waiter, with great servility, but appearances can be deceptive. 'Will that be all?'

'Yes, that's all, thanks. Thanks very much.' I know I'm approaching drunkenness and I make a concentrated effort to be civil. It is far better to be over-polite in a curry house than risk the wrath of the staff. Even the most innocent-looking curry has the potential to wreak awesome damage as it makes its bodily departure the following morning.

'Not at all, sir,' he says, fulfilling his half of the pretence, and I am left to watch my cigarette smoke ascend to the hypnotic tones of piped sitar music: snake charming, British style. Two young lads, also dressed in the customary white shirt and bow tie, chatted languidly to each other in some Indian language behind the tiny corner bar. I waved my empty lager bottle at them when I saw the waiter come through the kitchen door with my bhajees.

Now there is nothing but food, booze and fags, and I am preoccupied totally. All primary appetites will soon be satiated, and when the main course is served I am smiling like an idiot. My body has been denied the purge of an octane-calibre curry for a long time. The first few forkfuls, always the most painful, take a bottle and a half more lager to get through.

Understandably, this was going to be a bit of a shock to the system. It's been a while since I dared anything more than a madras. But after four or five bottles clearing my plate remained a feat no more possible than feasting on burning coal.

My mouth and throat were in flames of spice-shredded agony. Sweat patches were appearing on a shirt I'd already worn for three days, and my eyes stung wildly. It was as if I'd stuck my head into the centre of a small bonfire. I gave it a five-minute fag break, ordered another lager, and tried again. I put my knife and fork down for the last time a short while later. I had made no progress. I was beaten.

The boys at the bar had stopped talking. When I looked up I saw they were looking at me, and laughing.

'Would sir like some water?' one said.

'Get me the waiter!' I yelled. After a defiant pause one of them managed to mutter something round the kitchen door.

'What d'you call that?' I asked him when he arrived. 'I've been perfectly polite to you. Why'd you have to go and do something like that? I only wanted a vindaloo. I've been civil. Why'd you have to poison the fucking thing?'

'We give you vindaloo, sir. We stay open late to give you vindaloo,' said the waiter, gesturing to a room full of empty tables as if he didn't know what I was talking about.

'This isn't a vindaloo. That's fucking poison. It's napalm. Did I piss you off, did I?'

'Vindaloo is very hot curry, sir. Perhaps a madras or a korma next time,' he said, still calm. Smiling, almost.

'I know a vindaloo is a very hot curry. I eat them all the time. That is not a vindaloo. That is you taking the piss, it is you having a go, yeah?' I said, speaking as slowly as I could.

'I don't understand.'

'It's no wonder this fucking restaurant is empty,' I said, fishing my wallet from my trouser pocket. 'I hope you all go bust. Then we'll see how you behave

when the only job you can do is shat down the pan.'
I dropped a few tenners on the table and pushed him out of my way. I barely had to touch him. His small body sprang from my path like a gazelle.

As I opened the door one of the boys cried out to me.

'Sir. Is forty-two pounds. Is forty-two, sir.'

I stopped and looked at him for a long while. Nobody spoke. I took my wallet out again and dropped a tenner on the ground like it was a dirty tissue. Then I swore at them, slowly and deliberately, as if imparting words of great wisdom, and walked out, and kept walking.

By the time my rage subsided I was in Cotham, this hellish wind still blowing like a bastard, cold enough to cut through a gallon of beer, and God knows how long it would take to get back to the hotel, assuming I could find it. The pubs had all closed and there wasn't a taxi in sight. I was lost, wandering back streets I barely recognized. The important thing was to keep moving. Perhaps they had dosed my curry in the Bombay Sun. My evenings out always used to end up in the curry house. Bruce usually made a point of vindaloos all round and I had always been able to eat them, even the ones we asked them for especially, like the fahls and the tindaloos. But only now, lost and tired, with the cold air of the night on my teeth, was it a lot easier to remember I'd never really enjoyed a single one.

The streets I stumbled through that night were

affluent affairs, elegant starter homes for young, professional parents who'd already had all the start they needed. On every lawn rainwater pooled in the plastic hollows of upturned garden toys. Stickers on car windows said 'Save the Dolphins' and 'No Thanks!' to nuclear power. Not a light shone, not a soul stirred. They would never awake, it seemed, these streets whose citizens fought hard to find something to worry about.

The night would not get any better, although somewhere due west there was a resident's bar which served Bass and had a barman that called me sir. As luck had it I could see Cabot Tower from the end of the street. It kindled some sense of direction and I took a chance with the next left. Once I saw the top of the suspension bridge I knew I was on the home straight.

I followed the road around, Clifton village on my left, the unlit downs on my right and beyond them the Avon gorge. The bridge was strung with beads of white light like those mirrors in starlets' dressing rooms. Eleven jumpers last year, they reckon, but there were none out tonight. Not now, anyway. The Samaritans had placed a small ad in the vacant tollbooth: 'We're here to listen'.

The hotel doors were locked shut. Eventually I drew some old soldier out of his slumber, smoothing a few strands of unruly white hair with a tortoiseshell comb while he buttoned up what was obviously somebody's else's long blue overcoat with his other hand.

'You a resident?' he said, through the glass.

I showed him the key.

'Oh. Sorrysar!' he said, putting on his parade-ground patter, and after twisting the latch he held the door open for me.

'What took you so long?' I asked him, before he was tempted to salute.

'Hifyewdafusedthabell, sar,' he said, pointing a white-gloved finger at a fairly obvious button in a large brass surround.

'Oh,' I said. 'Bar still open?'

'Yessar.'

'Good.'

With that he shuffled out of sight to his sentry post. The boy behind reception was still there. He didn't say anything this time.

All the lights were off except the ones directly over the bar, where the barman was quietly occupying himself with one of the broadsheet crosswords. The suits had gone off to bed, saving themselves for their sales presentations in the morning, and the stools were up on their tables. I ordered a pint of Bass and asked whether there was anything to eat.

'Crisps or scampi fries,' the barman yawned. I had a packet of each.

Outside the long bay windows you could see the lights of Brunel's suspension bridge still shining, as they did throughout the night, every night of the year, like an advertisement for suicide. The jumpers were still staying away. It was too bloody cold to commit suicide tonight.

In the last century some posh daughter got knocked up and took the plunge, but she had one of those huge skirts that you see in the period dramas and it saved her life. All those hoops and straps turned the thing into a kind of parachute, slowing her fall. She's the sole survivor, or so the story goes: they say your heart stops before you hit the water. What was next for her? I wonder. A fresh start, or a hastily downed bottle of bleach? No coming back from that. I finished the scampi fries in one mouthful and drained my Bass. There are no fresh starts in this life.

The place was so quiet it was uncomfortable. One belch would wake the hotel. I whispered to the barman for a spare newspaper but he could only offer me the sports section, and even though I'd read it all in the White Hart I took it. It was just a little something to make me feel a little less out of place and I had trouble reading by this stage anyway.

'Triple brandy, please, with ice.'

'Yes, sir.'

There was no need to keep this man up. A triple would probably do it, or a couple of triples.

'World weariness,' said the barman abruptly, as I conquered my first brandy. 'Fatigued through tedium. Five letters. Begins with E.'

'I don't do crosswords,' I said. It was the last thing I can remember before I woke up fully dressed in my room, with the sunlight sneaking like a death ray through the curtains towards the bed.

I staggered into the windowless bathroom like a man in shell shock. The mirror above the sink did not reveal a pretty sight.

My face and tie were pebble-dashed with vindaloo. The tie I could take off; I rolled it up and slipped it into my jacket. I filled the sink with cold water and thrust my head into it, emptying my poor shrivelled lungs until I felt the last bubble of air dance up the side of my face. I could hear and feel nothing. It was extremely comfortable, only I couldn't breathe.

I wiped off the last of the curry, tucked in my shirt and lay back on the bed as still as I could with a clean, dry towel over my face. If I wasn't asleep again by the time my hair dried, I decided, I'd get up. I could have waited until it all fell out, it wouldn't have done any good. The world was turning now, and my stomach turned with it. At least I didn't have to pack.

I took the stairs on the way down, just to kid myself I'd taken some kind of exercise, and as I reached the final flight it struck me that I couldn't afford to pay the bar bill. I checked my wallet even though I already knew: I was right. I'd blown all of Declan's money down to a single tenner and some change.

Confusion reigned until I heard the sound of a girl's voice behind reception. The boy's shift had finished, which was only reasonable. The girl couldn't know who I was, how long I was booked in for, or that I had no luggage. I could calmly hand over the key and walk out. Feigning nonchalance, I strolled in.

The girl in reception, as it happened, said nothing and cared less. Sitting there and smiling all day was a grim enough task as it was. She had a fantastic smile, actually. A pretty young girl hasn't smiled at me like that since I was a young man myself, with an unsullied record. Didn't mean anything, of course, just a special talent on her part, but it's been twenty odd years since someone smiled at me like that for a reason. I fled the lobby before I thought of her.

It was just as well. Not a shade past eight o'clock and the car was already being eyed up by one of the council's finest, meandering up the meters, ticket machine in hand. I beat him to it but he wasn't to be deterred. He was just stepping off the pavement for a patronizing chat when I shifted gear and was gone, leaving him to talk to a few cubic feet of carbon monoxide: not a bad start to the day.

Nothing, unfortunately, is so simple. In an unmarked at the end of the road sat Julian Gilboursen, clutching a polystyrene cup of coffee with his white uniform shirt on. He was one of the policemen I'd known in the days when Bruce was alive, and he knew about the ban and he knew about my statement. He wouldn't hesitate to pull me up.

I sank into my seat and kept going. It has to be said, I rarely panic. My reflexes are so poor that by the time I sense any danger the threat has usually passed. In any case, it was too late to stop and turn around. He didn't see me, or at least I didn't catch him looking: they are all far from unobservant people. Once I turned the corner I put my foot to the floor but it was useless. Traffic had congealed in the streets like cold gravy. It took me over half an hour to get from Clifton Triangle to anywhere near Dixon's place of work. I kept expecting to see the unmarked in the rear-view but he hadn't followed me. Caxton House backed on to Redcliffe Mead, a quiet side street with meter-free parking spaces, and I grabbed one. The Bell wasn't twenty yards up the road, which I knew would prove tempting once open, but this was work, for now.

I took the chance before the day began to nip down to the garage by the flyover and load up on provisions. It was within walking distance. The flyover was only ever meant to be a temporary affair, but it's overshadowed the surrounding buildings for as long as anyone can remember. Its creaking metal skeleton is one of the city's landmarks now, and is usually referred to with fondness. Strange what people can get used to.

The garage was owned by one of the supermarket chains and so it had a large shop attached. I loaded up on sandwiches, pasties, pork pies, crisps, soft drinks, wine gums, newspapers and cigarettes. Seeing they had a licence I bought two cans of cider too, just in case I felt like it. It will all be consumed today, if not from hunger then merely to pass the time. After all, today I am being paid to sit in a car for what will probably be about fourteen hours.

There is very little to be said about this kind of work. It is easy to imagine. There are no hidden depths to it. There are no amusing anecdotes. You get to sit down, you get to stay warm, and as long as you keep your eyes open and your head down you can do whatever you want.

As I have almost always done throughout my entire adult life, I missed the nine o'clock start. So on the way back, arms full of cellophaned snacks, I ducked into the office's basement car park. His car was there, or at least a black Honda Civic was, almost directly opposite the entrance, reversed in so it was pointing outward for when he left. Not everyone can be bothered to do that, I think. Then I went and sealed myself in.

I hopped radio stations for the first two hours. Eventually I left it on Radio 4, which was broadcasting a crappy drama about environmentalists in the Lake District, and wondered what it would be like to stake out a real criminal instead of somebody's hapless husband. I rolled down the window and smoked, if only to relieve the smell of yesterday's curry. I read the newspaper and chewed my wine gums. I emptied a litre bottle of Coke. I ate a BLT and a sausage roll. I stayed fucking put. Litter gathered at my feet like leaves at the base of an autumnal tree. Time struggles by. Nothing happens.

After two and a half hours I turn the radio off.

Any longer and the battery will give out. In another hour I have finished the newspapers. After four hours I am reduced to reading the lonely hearts in the *Evening Herald*. Most of these, it is said, are submitted by unfaithful spouses, and while one or two came straight out and admitted it there was nothing in the other generic, acronym-filled ads to tell you either way. I scan the faces at the midday outflow but it looks like Mr Dixon is working lunch today.

After five hours I need to piss. Now I could nip down the Bell, and assuming I didn't stop for a pint I'd be back in under two minutes. Not long, but it only takes thirty seconds for him to disappear to destinations unknown while I'm left standing with my dick in my hand. I hold it for another thirty minutes, just to keep myself occupied, and then I reach for the empty pop bottle. No matter how tight you screw the lid back on you can still smell it.

By mid-afternoon I have resorted to mind games. I try to name a country and a capital for every letter of the alphabet. I name all the pubs in South Bristol from Hotwells to Hanham. I remember where the beer comes from: Smiles in Bristol, Brains in Cardiff, Abbey in Bath, Moles in Melksham, Wadworth in Devizes. I drift. Doing this sort of thing gets easier as you get older.

In another hour or two I will at least be able to drive for a short while. Even the hard-working Mr Dixon must admit defeat and face the horrors of home eventually. I don't mind the wait. Some people's work can give them something they can take home: status, wealth, camaraderie, some sort of satisfaction. You have to use your imagination to feel pleased about this job, but it's work nonetheless, even if it is fucking some ineffectual middle manager arse over tit.

Then it's gone five, with the day fading fast. Cars emerge from the basement, nudging into the stationary ranks to steal an inch every couple of seconds as they pull and jerk their way across town. I can see it all from the quiet refuge of my empty side street. In ten thousand suburban semi-detacheds ten thousand weeknight dinners are being slid into ovens. Ten thousand schoolchildren are sauntering back from school, ten thousand satchels dropped in hallways and ten thousand televisions suddenly switched to blaring life. The veins and the arteries of this city are blocked with lives. At least I don't take up any space.

Half past seven and none of the cars that left was Dixon's. The lights are still on, although all I can see from this angle is the foam-tiled ceiling and the tops of over-sized pot plants. He's in there somewhere, poring over reams of printed paper or hunched over a computer, whatever people do in a proper job.

By half past eight I know either something odd is going on or I've let him go. I leave the car to stand outside and smoke; it's not well lit and I will draw no attention. Tenser than I realized, I found myself crossing and recrossing the street, barely able to walk after so much time in the car. I was creaking more than the flyover. The logical thing to do would have been to check his parking place, but I didn't want to know. I'd rather have rotted ignorantly in the street than face another failure over something so simple. After all, I had wine gums and cigarettes left for a good few hours yet. But by nine I managed to steel myself and headed rampward, down into the depths of the car park.

There was nothing there. The space was empty. I tore around the rest of the car park hoping it'd been moved to a different bay, then someone's yelling at me, God knows who, and I'm scanning frantically for a black Civic with a mild sweat on and an unwanted certainty looming. There's only one floor. It's mostly empty. His car is gone.

It is not something I can fully appreciate in an instant, and before despair swarms in there's a heavy hand on my shoulder. You can tell by the weight of it that it knows what it's about. I turn, almost expecting to get the other one in my face, but it is only security introducing himself, some gym freak with a body like an upturned pear.

'What are you doing here?'

'My dog,' I say spontaneously, out of breath and agitated. And with good cause, but not the cause he has in mind.

'Come again?'

'My dog ran in here. A Yorkshire terrier. A pit

bull went after him and he scarpered. I saw him go down here.'

'Well, you can't just run around down here after him. This is private property.'

'Is there another exit?'

'Yeah. Just round that corner,' he said, nodding in the direction of what I'd thought was another parking bay.

'Oh.' It was all the noise I could make.

'I'm going to have to ask you to leave,' he said. I've no idea how many times that's been said to me. There was never any point in arguing.

'OK, sod him,' I said, showing a sudden change of heart which security seemed happy enough to accept.

'You should get yourself a proper bloody dog anyway, mate,' he shouted out as I was going.

I hunched down on the pavement by my car and leant back against a cold brick wall, watching what was left of my breath condense in front of me. Somehow I was not surprised by any of this. I was angry, though, that I let it happen, or that I thought it wouldn't. I don't know. It seemed that I couldn't do anything in those free-falling days that followed Bruce and McKellan. It seemed bitterly funny that I'd thought of it as work at all, especially when I'd never really wanted any of it in the first place. None of it. I felt sick.

I knew then what I had really believed all along: there was no way of avoiding or postponing what I had been hired to do. Leaving the car where it was, I set off on foot in the direction of the river. I had seen enough of it for the time being, and if it got nicked I could always say I'd left something valuable under the seat and claim it on the insurance.

To get to the river you have to walk through the council flats, the usual tower blocks covered in washing and satellite dishes, the greenery between them a wasteland. I wonder whether they ever got round to asking themselves about their drawing-board utopia, those fifties planners, about the arrival of that ugly, barren space that now inexplicably forms the collective front garden of four or five thousand people. We live too far apart, these days, to live this close together. On the other side of the tower blocks creeps the ever slow and mud-steady Avon. On the other side of that lies Bedminster. It is not a pretty stretch of water.

There is an old cast-iron footbridge that you can cross about five minutes westward. I don't see another soul until I make it into Bedminster, and there the usual suspects are out earning their title.

Every pane in the phone box has been smashed. I entered and found myself standing on a carpet of broken glass that chimed every time I shifted my weight. I put in some change and listened to the sound of my own breathing, of glass breaking, and a phone ringing in the doubtlessly well-furnished living room of the Dixons' marital home. Over the road I could see seagulls perching on the upturned chassis of an abandoned Escort protruding from the mud banks, revealed by the river at its lowest ebb.

'Mrs Dixon?' I must do this now before I just chuck the whole project in altogether. That would be the easiest thing to do.

'Speaking,' she said.

'Robin Llywelyn here.' I had expected, I realized, the spontaneous formation of some believable excuse, but nothing occurred to me. As it turned out, none was needed.

'You took a considerable risk ringing me at home, you know,' she said. 'But then he is bedridden. I didn't realize when we agreed to this that I was going to end up being the observer.'

'Sorry?' I said, still not understanding a word, feeling only the sensation of a rug being pulled sharply from under my feet.

'He's ill, Mr Lou-Ellen. He's been bedridden since he drove back to the house. The flu, I believe. I trust you saw him drive back to the house. You didn't spend all day outside the house, did you? I didn't see you.'

'No,' I said, slack jawed. I have always been able to sound indifferent when life pulls a fast one; for a while I interpreted this inertness as stoicism. 'Of course not.'

'I would have rung your secretary only she wasn't in the office.'

'No, flu too, actually.'

'It's doing the rounds.'

'I know.' Fate had decreed I should keep my incompetence to myself, or so it seemed.

'Now listen, Lou-Ellen. I think he's going to be bedridden for a couple of days, and you know as well as I do that even if he was up and about this surveillance idea of yours is going to get us nowhere. I want you to forget it, like I said, and start concentrating on fixing him up. There's a perfect opportunity to do it this weekend, in fact, so are you going to do our job or not?'

Yeah, I'd do it. I was too amazed to say anything else. As long as certain conditions were met, of course.

'We have yet to fully discuss the . . . remuneration.' There was no use talking around it, I wasn't up to a pitch.

'Well?'

'Fifteen grand.' I plucked it, outrageously, out of the blue. Now it was her turn to pause.

'Fifteen thousand pounds?'

'Yeah.' She could take it or leave it. By now I was past caring. If I got the job I'd probably fuck it up anyway.

'Fine,' she said.

'OK. I'll ring you tomorrow.' It dawned on me much later that I was only ever to talk to this woman in short bursts. It was always very draining, for one reason or another. 'Ten o'clock all right?'

'Yes, and I don't know how you can expect to be taken seriously without a mobile phone.'

Unbelievable, I thought, and started walking

before disbelief could root me to the spot. She was as gullible as the rest of them: fifteen grand, for fuck's sake. Even I could change my life for the better with fifteen grand, and this Dixon character was going to get himself fucked over sooner or later. He had that kind of face. It might as well be me. Why not?

At the top of Bedminster, alongside the river on Coronation Road, there is an Irish pub called the Grosvenor Arms. I was walking past it now. I hadn't had a beer all day, and the prospect of a pint came to me like a holy vision. I was standing right outside it, and the thick condensation on the windows told me that it was busy and it was warm.

CHAPTER 4

I have always, always regretted going in the Grosvenor Arms, every time I've been in the place. I have frequented worse pubs, and my criteria are hardly extensive, but the Grosvenor disturbs me. They're all Irish, and I am not. Maybe that's all it is; I keep the company I do because it is all I have, and to be a stranger in any pub around here is to be a stranger everywhere. This is my part of town, the city's lowest common denominator, and the lean and lonely years have taught me there is nowhere else to go.

Sometimes they stuck a band in the corner but people usually ignored them after the first few numbers, and by the end of the evening they usually didn't have enough elbow room to play. There was a band tonight, although you'd strain to hear it over the volume of the conversation.

It is not the place to go for a quiet pint. There was hardly space to stand any night of the week, band or no, and you'd get the old eight-hundred-years-of-oppression rant until your ears bled if you weren't careful. If you didn't answer back they'd leave off eventually, but it would start up again within the hour. Being Welsh, I suppose I was spared the worst of it.

I fought my way back to the bar and pointed to the Carlsberg pump. The barman stuck his hand out and I put two quid in it. I took my plastic glass to a spot of spare wall by the front door. It was draughty, but I stood a better chance of being left alone.

The place hadn't changed: a good half-a-dozen Celtic posters on the walls, and a few more framed photos of Gaelic football teams. There were road signs for places like Skibbereen and Castlecomer, don't ask me where they were. Some heated words were being exchanged at the nearest table but it was difficult to dissect the context from the general hubbub. Something about the North. I was listening to a similar conversation in here when I heard about a story far more serious, and here I am again. I never learn. This is where I found out who killed Bruce, or at least where I found out who was directly responsible, whose hands delivered the blow.

Detective Inspector William Cookson, or Bruce to his friends. His family decided to chuck it in and emigrate, and then his mother decided to chuck it in and come back, bringing Bruce with her. He still talked with traces of an Australian accent. Not the most imaginative nickname, but there you go. These are policemen we're talking about.

Bruce and I were regulars at the same pub once, a long time ago. The Bank, actually, around by

Frogmore Street station. I don't go there any more. Great lad, he was. Introduced me to a few other police friends of his and then, more or less, I was one of the gang. More or less.

It was Bruce who got McKellan to take me on. The area manager at the collection agency I was working for had started to kill leads on heavy debtors for backhanders, telling head office they were untraceable if they could give him a little bit of cash in hand. It wouldn't have been so bad but we had to meet the targets set by head office by coming down on the small fry, people who wouldn't complain if you took a few liberties because they didn't know any better. I got very bitter one night after a skinful, listening to tall tales of police triumph and criminal defeat after another day of doorstepping and climbing through kitchen windows, and poured it all out.

'I'll sort it,' Bruce had said, 'I'll fix the bastard, don't you worry. And I'll get you something else to do.'

Bruce and McKellan were not the sort you'd expect to get along, and they didn't. I don't know what favours they could have owed each other but Bruce got me out of debt collecting. It was a job, apparently, that had proven my investigative abilities, and he landed me a spot working for McKellan. It sounded too good to be true at the time, and of course it was. The only people who can hand you an invitation to join the good guys are the angels, and even they require faith, and death, and a blameless life. Couldn't even meet them halfway there, couldn't or wouldn't. Back then, though, I thought my chance had come, as if being good and being lucky were somehow related.

A few months later I came across the area manager one night in Brislington. He spotted me and came straight over, started mouthing off about an Australian policeman who he said had tried to hit on him for money.

'What did you do?' I asked.

'Told him to fuck off, of course, the little cunt.'

I didn't pay him that much attention. Bruce had probably gone in there and hauled him over the coals in front of his staff, and he must have felt he had to say something to me, for the sake of his dignity. He'd known Bruce and I were friends, and so he came up with a load of bullshit about him and what happened. I hadn't been there, so I didn't know, but that was what I reckoned it was about. Then Bruce appeared at my flat, although I'd never given him my address, and left a locked suitcase there. He left a few more, over the months, and sometimes very unsavoury characters turned up to collect them. I didn't object; it didn't seem much of an imposition, considering the strings he'd pulled on my behalf. So it seemed at the time. Then there was a knock at the door one night and it wasn't Bruce at all but two police officers I'd never seen, and they took me down to the station. Until then I hadn't really thought about it, and the next thing I was squealing like a pig.

It's like believing your horoscope: people always pick the easiest option. Take that Japanese soldier they found decades after the war, holed up on some island with a broken machine gun and a handful of rusty bullets. We shouldn't be surprised by the heights of his fanaticism but rather by the depth of the hungry space underneath it, by his need to believe. In everyday life truth is something that follows the path of least resistance, and the harshest of physical adaptations are nothing compared to the metaphysical. It was far easier for someone like him to spend twenty years alone in the jungle, I'm sure, than to go back to his father's corner shop in Nagoya and sell prophylactics to GIs. Not that he won, in the end. They still found him.

I will never know what Bruce was really up to. When they started the internal investigation they took him off the regional crime squad and he began chasing other work. You couldn't expect a man like that to just slot back into the old Avon Constabulary. He became involved in anti-terrorist activity with parts of the security forces, or so the story goes. He died in a car bomb on Royal Oak Avenue in 1982.

Two years later I was in here, where no one knows me, and someone was boasting about it. Just a passing pint on my part, pure coincidence, but he was saying things which weren't exactly in the public domain. Like what part of the car the bomb was in, and so on. If he hadn't killed Bruce he knew enough about it, at any rate. I made sure I popped in a few times a fortnight. You couldn't let something like that lie. The man was from Mayo, I found out, and his name was Michael O'Connell.

I told Knight, the new DI, and he was more surprised than anything that I'd got to him first; me, an untrained civilian. He was shocked, in fact, but when he found out it was more luck than judgement he started to take me seriously. He told me not to worry, that he'd take care of it, and that I shouldn't mention it to anyone else again.

Even so, I kept coming. I didn't see what harm it could do, and then one night shortly after O'Connell stopped visiting the Grosvenor Arms, and every other pub around here. I never saw him again. Unless he got wise and did a bunk, or met some other end, I knew he was out there some- where, under several feet of ready-mixed cement or country soil, taken care of. It was not what I'd intended. There was never any attempt to prose- cute him or even investigate; my word, Knight had said, was good enough for him. And I never did mention it to anyone else.

A few weeks after that I stopped coming here myself. What with one thing and another I'd lost interest in the whole affair, in everything. I was drinking whatever and wherever I could by that stage, now Bruce was dead and McKellan had sloped off with a body full of tumours to follow suit. The job changed a lot after that, once I had to fend for myself.

I don't feel like staying but I battle to the bar for another Carlsberg: by the time I reached another pub they'd have called last orders. Some pissed idiot in a donkey jacket clamps a hand the size of a shovel head on my shoulder and smiles, but I squirm away before any favours are asked and find my safe spot in the doorway still going free. The drunks in there asked for money all the time. No one cared. People in there have insulted me for not lending drunks money.

It would have been cold, standing there like a human doormat, had it not been for the mass of people crammed in behind me. The frosted glass in the window revealed only the vaguest outlines of the city outside. You couldn't tell where the rooftops ended and the sky began.

I drank quickly, trying to get my mind off the memories the place raised, and all I was left with was the loss I made at Greenways the previous day. It was the act of someone twenty years younger. To be my age and get sucked in by something like that, well, it's either stupidity or desperation, one or the other. I don't think I'm stupid. I have fucked up massively, plenty of times, but I still don't think you could call me thick. I am only too aware of the stupidity of my actions, or most of them, which has to be some indication of intelligence.

Desperation, then, was the only other answer. How or why or what for I couldn't begin to say, not then. It was the first time I'd asked myself the question, the first time I'd sensed something hiding in my days that wasn't there before. I must be desperate, I thought. After all, there must be some reason why the usual distractions no longer seem to work.

There was only one thing I could say with any certainty at that point. There, alone in a room full of gibbering Irishmen, with the day spent sitting pointlessly in a parked car, with nowhere to sleep but the floor of my office, I became acutely aware that there was something specific and fundamentally wrong either with my life or everyone else's. Neither alternative pleased me particularly.

PART II

ENTRAPMENT

CHAPTER 1

That night I slept in the car. I'd only intended to fetch the two cans of cider but I drank them where I found them, and after that the office seemed a long way off. I awoke in the middle of the night to see the windows frozen inside and out, chewing on the stench of old sweat and a dozen other bad smells. Cold air is not always fresh air. I took the bottle of piss and hurled it into the darkness.

I tried sleeping with the seat back and my feet on the dash. I tried lying across the back seat. I flipped down the back seats so I could curl up in the boot. Nothing worked. A sleep so light it could have been a fine mist fell about four, far too late to make much of a difference. It lasted until a little after half five, when a milk float hummed past on its electric engine, its bottles clinking chirpily as it went. I was so angry I would have wrenched the milkman off and driven it into the river, but the things have no speed and he could easily have caught up with me.

The engine started eventually and I put the heaters on full, which was daft. I should have given the fan time to warm because it was just as cold as everything else and the blast hit me like frost-bite. I shivered and watched the thin layer of ice inside the windscreen slowly melt and dribble into the dashboard. I got her moving and gradually the Rover thawed.

The sun hadn't even risen yet, and all I wanted was a decent night's kip in my own bed, a shower, a shave, and a clean set of clothes. Normally it was in my power to avail myself of these things. Why, I asked, am I awake at half five in the morning, half ill, tired, foul breathed, bearded, and thirsty? I would have kicked my front door down but I couldn't afford a new one. I promised myself as soon as I had some money the first thing I'd do would be to ring a locksmith.

I made a few aimless laps of the empty city on roads that were for once clear enough to allow for third gear and above. Nowhere was even open. There was over an hour yet before the first pyjama'd commuter would stagger bleary eyed into his bathroom to run his toothbrush under the tap. The day had yet to start, for those whose days still started and ended. Mine seemed to have merged into a single, rushing stream, and life came one shrinking handful at a time. Yet I am not alone. There are others, and there is always somewhere.

I have come to know this corner of the world too well for it to close its doors to me completely. Under a bridge by the Cumberland Basin there was a transport canteen that probably hadn't closed since it had first opened for business. It was a start, I thought, rounding Baltic Wharf. It was another place I hadn't been to for years. I left the car between a couple of tarpaulined flatbeds awaiting their units.

The canteen was two adjoining Portakabins raised from the damp tarmac on a platform of breeze blocks. The breakfast was fried, except for the beans, and served in heaps on hubcapsized plates with a free mug of tea or coffee. It cost less than a pair of pints. The place was dotted with truckers tucking in, and talk was hushed. Few people knew each other and no one was fully awake. I recognized one of them, although he didn't seem to recognize me.

A fair-headed guy with a couple of earrings in each ear and sunken eyes. He was one of the faces that used to appear at my door every so often for the odd suitcase or sports bag Bruce had me keeping for collection, and even then he looked like he was in the terminal stages of some wasting disease. He had a face stretched so tight across his narrow skull you expected it to snap like elastic at any moment. By the look of things he was doing nothing more these days than selling speed to truckers, maybe a wrap at a time. Together with the dole and the housing allowance this probably got him by.

If any of these truckers were going Continental

there'd be takers. How else can you do a week's driving in seventy-two straight hours? It worked quite well, so I hear, as long as you were sensible. Otherwise you ended up in a lay-by somewhere biting back tears while the paranoia subsided enough for you to keep your hands on the wheel.

He was too oblivious or discreet to meet my gaze, and perhaps he didn't remember me anyway, but in an interview room in Frogmore Street I had described him in detail not once but three times to the two police officers who tried to take Bruce down. It hadn't done either of us any favours, by the looks of things. He and I were the only non-truckers in the room, save the cook, and I suspect from his saddlesore gait that he had been behind the wheel once himself.

It didn't seem a bad life. Not only did their vehicles have beds in them, they always had somewhere to go and they always knew how to get there. When the tachometer tells them the day's driving is done they can do whatever they want, as long as the engine revs again come morning. It has a certain clarity, knowing exactly what freedom you have and how you are restrained. As far as the answers to life's questions are concerned, people have looked in worse places than the road atlas and a copy of *Razzle*. All just an HGV licence away, but that's a new trick and I am no longer such a youthful pooch. Very possibly the dealer was thinking the same thing.

The food was stodge but it was edible. It would

have to be, for lorry drivers are an intolerant lot, although why they kept coming back here was beyond me. The stove that ran the whole length of the rear wall was covered in the black lard of endless breakfasts. It was easier to imagine the mountains crumbling into the sea than this bubbling conveyor belt of cholesterol ever stopping. The world would surely cease spinning before the bacon stopped spitting, or the Daddy's sauce ran dry, or anyone ever did a proper job of the washing up. I mean, I'm a disgrace in the kitchen myself, but how one cook could produce this much grime from only food seemed like a feat of fucking alchemy.

I wiped the white Formica table with the edge of my hand, watching the grease collect in my palm, while my reflection stared dully up at me from the cleanish streak of table-top I had created. It looked to me like a face that, in its own way, also belonged to a man who had done a lot of bad things. To look at the dealer and me you could actually believe that bullshit about getting the face you deserve, and although we had a year or two yet before reaching Orwell's magic half-century, we were definitely on course: he was hawking his little clingfilm bags, and I was somebody you went to if you wanted your husband fitted up with another woman.

The wives got set up too, but that wasn't my speciality. They went to someone else for that, someone with a better idea of how female desire functioned. I only knew about the places where men looked for what was missing, and things went missing all the time. Fifteen or thirty years of marriage, it seemed, was no protection. It is a knowledge for which I paid a certain price, and I am entitled to charge a certain fee. Money doesn't judge, or differentiate, though at one time I'd have taken a truncheon to someone like me, if they'd decided I'd been worthy of carrying one.

I had another coffee, and then another. There were several indifferent hours to expend before I said I'd ring Mrs Dixon again. I would have gone for a walk along the docks but the weather wasn't conducive to outdoor thinking. I needed to get my head straight, and there's only so much caffeine you can take before the babbling begins, no matter how tired you are. I got back into the car and drove to the office.

The city was already beginning to clog on the first of the morning horde. I left the car outside Greenways so I didn't have to wait at the lights and half jogged (it wasn't far) up to the office door to minimize exposure. It was a wasted effort: the office was equally chilly, and once I was in I was nearly running on the spot. It was too cold to stand still.

I'd have gone into immediate hibernation only the rug/blanket was covered in ash from Tuesday's spillage, and the rest of the place was nearly as bad. I was so pissed off with myself that before

I knew it I was rooting around for the vacuum cleaner, and then I remembered that Maggie always brought it in, so my spontaneous urge to clean vanished about as quickly as it appeared, which was customary. She'd been nagging me to buy my own Hoover for months. I made do with taking the rug out into the lobby and shaking its contents out there as best I could, thus making both parts of the office dirty, which was more my sort of style. As an afterthought I grabbed a memo from the pad and stuck a do-not-disturb sign on the door in case Maggie returned. Then I bedded down under the radiator, but sleep wouldn't come.

I gave it over an hour down there, tossing and turning and ceiling-staring until the patterns in the Artex started to move. Sleep had left me, for now, and would not be returning in the near future. I wasn't even that tired, I just wanted to lie down and forget about things, and I couldn't. I was faced with the ignominy of consciously witnessing yet more of my limited hours slide meaninglessly by, and there was no way of hiding from them, nowhere to avert my eyes from the inevitable destruction of another day. As soon as half eight lumbered round I nipped downstairs for some fags and a paper.

By nine I was back on the coffee and soldiering through a pack of cigarettes. Maggie was still being ill, evidently. I grabbed the directory and rang a few locksmiths, just to get quotes, but it was all academic unless you had cash. Most people would ring their landlord or their letting agency, but mine had been kind or negligent enough to let me slip a month or two behind in the rent, and I didn't want to bother them. I had already clogged up their helpline with plenty of post-pub late-night calls about fuck-all in the past. Until I knew what my movements were I couldn't say when I'd be available to meet them either, so I opened my phone book to Mrs Dixon's number and watched the hands tick and tock their way around the clock. Then I held my breath and dialled.

'Well, these are the details,' she announced, cutting the usual pleasantries a little short. 'He has a conference in the Hilton this Saturday.'

'You want to go for it?'

'It's the perfect opportunity. I want this over with as soon as possible.'

'It's important not to hurry these things, Mrs Dixon. If the girl screws up he might get suspicious, and that could blow our chances of a second attempt. For a while, at least, anyway.'

'I know. That's why I want to meet the girl.'

My silence demanded an explanation more eloquently than I ever could.

'I want to know that you've got the right material for the job. I'll know that better than anyone.'

'Are you sure about this?' I said. It had happened once before. The wife just flipped, slapped the girl around and called her all kinds of things. Couldn't handle the reality of the situation. I get plenty of clients who pull out, dormice flirting with some idea of equality or warhorses toying with the power.

'Absolutely. I know him and I know what he likes. I don't want you to pick up some lice-ridden whore. You're going to need someone young and attractive and intelligent. Plastic jewellery, fake leather and needle marks will not prove a temptation for my husband.'

'Of course,' I said, but you never know, with a wife like that. Probably jump at the chance. Probably insist on paying the girl himself if he found out. It is hard to imagine bedtime in the Dixon household as a passionate or even sweaty affair, and that sort of girl would be cheaper too, but I kept these thoughts to myself.

'I'm glad you can understand that,' she said, not sounding particularly glad at all. 'What will your next step be?'

'Well . . .' I began, slowly, feeling like I was being tested. 'The room needs to be booked as soon as possible. Then I'll put in an audio bug perhaps, nothing complicated.'

'Audio?' she asked.

'Yeah. That should do it.'

'You can't get anything, you know, visually?'

'I could do. You mean photos?'

'No, I was thinking video. I think if we got it on video we'd have a pretty compelling package. I want all the stops pulled out on this. I want maximum impact.'

'So you want it on video?' I asked, desperately.

'Yes.'

'Well, don't worry. I've done it all before,' I lied. 'I know a place in St Pauls where I can pick that up. Shouldn't be too much of a problem. Better get that room booked from Friday, though, so I have time to install it all.'

'All right. How long will it take to find the right girl?'

'I can get her today, probably.' They weren't hard to find, whoever or whatever you wanted. It was the wanting that was the key, rather than thinking idly about it whenever the mood took you, and I had the lure of a large fee to drag me through the selection process. With that at my back I knew I was bound to come up with somebody.

'In that case you can meet me at the Hilton this evening.'

'Make it late,' I said. No point in putting yourself out. 'After half ten, say. These girls are easier to find in the dark.'

'As you wish.'

'I'll be needing more of that cash up front, I'm afraid.'

'Oh, really?'

'Yeah. These video systems aren't cheap. Five thousand should do it.' It was only one third of the overall fee. Large advances are not uncommon in this industry. 'Could you bring it round this afternoon?'

There were, I confess, better ways of putting this across. Mrs Dixon made a point of laughing and snorting for a good ten seconds. 'I'm not going to pay you a penny more, Lou-Ellen, until the job is done.'

'That's highly unorthodox for a job of this nature,' I said, attempting a defence.

'Then I must be a highly unorthodox woman. I consider the down payment I have made to be sufficient, and if you do not, then I will simply take my business elsewhere.'

'There's no need to do that, Mrs Dixon,' I cooed, back-pedalling. I kowtowed some more, loud and clear so there would be no confusion, and we hung up. The thing was, I really needed the money.

Five grand was no exaggeration. I had looked into this before. That sort of equipment would put you at the premium end of the market, but I'd never been able to afford it. Now it looked like I finally was working at the premium end of the market, and a few photos weren't going to be enough: this woman wanted something that would shame his whole family.

I did consider the alternatives first. There was the possibility of putting a normal camcorder somewhere, or hiding in the room with it, or booking an adjacent room and drilling some kind of hole. They were all impractical, or bigger risks than I could afford to take, and for the first time in my entire life I rang my bank and asked for an appointment with the manager. The worst they could do was laugh.

'What does it concern?' said the woman on the other end of the phone, who then explained there was no need to bother the manager with a simple loan. They had credit supervisors to deal with that sort of thing.

'So when can I see a credit supervisor?' I asked. Credit supervisors turned out to be pretty elusive creatures too, and none was available until the beginning of the following week, although there was a slot free at midday if I could make it. It could be done: I had a little over two hours to remove all traces of the last few days' events from my body. The flat was still out of bounds but there were no clean clothes there anyway, and I have grown used to coping with these kinds of circumstances, this sudden compulsory whiplash back into a projected respectability.

Maggie had left her cardigan draped over the chair behind the desk in the lobby, and there was seventy quid in it, I remembered, together with her library card and a small pair of scissors. She was in the early stages of her dotage and had started leaving things all over the place, and it bemused me, I suppose, to see someone more out of sorts than myself, so I'd been watching her closely. I had thought seriously about taking the money before, but with no real reason to I couldn't bring myself to do it. Now I took it with the transitory guilt of a wayward teen stealing from his own mother, knowing she would forget it was ever there, and I told myself that if her flu continued a get-well card was the least I could do.

I could buy a razor, foam, shampoo, a towel, new socks, new underwear, a new shirt and a new tie. I could buy a brush for getting the lint off my suit. I could buy shoe polish. For seventy quid, I could make myself a new man. I would need all that stuff sooner or later, I told myself, so it might as well be now. To be honest I'd needed it for years, but had never somehow been able to justify even this paltry domestic expenditure.

I didn't have time to go into town and back but at the other end of Wells Road there was a shopping centre that had everything I wanted. I spent five minutes waiting for a bus, which was all I could wait, and it didn't come so I began the steep trek up to the Merrywells shopping centre on foot. Before I'd walked fifty yards, of course, the bus pulled past me with its cargo of content, sedentary passengers.

I ran to catch it at the next stop but it only took a few footsteps to teach me I was being naive. Those days are past me too now, my body has started to live on its own terms, and its present contract with me is far less mutual than its previous one. I consoled myself with another fag, smoking spitefully as I dragged myself on. I was only mildly dizzy when Merrywells' forebidding silhouette began to loom in the middle distance, a faceless concrete cube that looked like something from downtown Murmansk. No queues for bread, but I'm sure everything else is right on the button: pebble-dash, concrete, dark stairwells rank with piss, the cheapest chains of clothes shops, travel agents whose holidays seem less appealing than working, off-licences selling paint-stripper liquor in fancy bottles and strange, frightening shops that sell things like china puppy spectacle-holders and fridge magnets of the Eiffel Tower, all for one pound. Here is consumerism without the veneer, without the gloss. And we all need a bit of gloss. This is a tad brutal even for here.

Fifteen thousand pounds would make no difference at all up here. It would be tragic, in fact, to have five digits in the bank and still end up queuing at the checkout in SupaSava with a basket full of obscure own-brand groceries, yet where else can I go? For the briefest of moments I wonder for the first time how much good the money from this job will really do me: that's how bad it is, shopping in Merrywells.

Despite, or because of, this, the place got by in terms of trade. However shoddy, however useless and unwanted the goods on offer, they were all bargains, just like their Day-Glo price tags said they were, and there would always be a substratum of the market there to buy them. I got everything I wanted, or something close, and still had change from seventy quid. And I did pick a get-well card out at random for Maggie, just to keep her sweet.

I managed to catch the bus on the way back,

which saved me badly needed time. There were fourteen frantic minutes before midday. I was straight into the toilet and running the sink while I unwrapped a bar of soap. There was no warm water, I realized fearfully after I'd stripped to my waist, but it had to be done. Waiting for the sink to fill, looking down at my flabby pale chest, I couldn't help the feeling that it somehow deserved it.

There was no mirror either, but a root-around in Maggie's desk produced the compact she used when covering up the canyons that age had carved in her face, and I took a plastic disposable razor out of its multi-pack. It wasn't going to be the closest shave, but it has never been something I've excelled at. There are ingrowing hairs on my neck that always seem to draw blood. Quite often I shaved only every other day, even when the facilities were at hand, and I have struggled unsuccessfully with beards for periods. For whatever reason, this simple manly skill has always evaded me.

My new shirt was your bog-standard white polyester variety, and straight out of the polythene it felt fresh on the skin, or at least it did for about twenty seconds, although I think the experience may still have been worth it. The tie was navy with a family crest that someone had probably dreamt up on the back of an envelope two minutes into the production meeting.

I had no brush or comb but what hair I had was

damp enough to be shaped by hand to an acceptable level of presentability. I tore apart one of Maggie's magazines and, prompted by the seriousness of the occasion, began polishing my shoes. There are those, of course, for whom shiny shoes are a potent symbol of order. I am aware of the danger inherent in this fallacy, and this is one of the better reasons why my footwear was caked in mud that took some time to remove.

Then, job done with the best of a bad lot, it was off bankward without time spare to check the clock. I knew I'd be late. It didn't stop me trying, and I mounted Windmill Hill at a pace so brisk I could have taken off at the summit. This, admittedly, on the part of a man who hadn't broken into a jogging pace for over two years, but it's no exaggeration to say that when I turned into Bedminster Parade I felt like a sprinter breaking the finish line. Ducking into Barclays twenty minutes late I asked politely for Martin, lungs smouldering like seabed volcanoes under the tar of a million fags, and collapsed on to one of the seats that lined the walls.

'I don't know,' sighed a sad-looking woman. 'You're very late. I'll see if he's still able to see you.' Then she tapped a code out on a keypad and went into the office. I was the only customer in the entire place. There was only one cashier at the windows and she was busy reading something beneath the counter. I strained to hear any kind of activity and heard nothing, except myself, who sounded like a man slowly dying at moderate volume. A glance in a strip of mirror among the light wood panelling on the opposite side of the room told me that whatever presentability I'd achieved had been undone by the struggle to appear only twenty minutes late.

After five minutes, during which I suppose I am expected to believe desperate pleas were made on my behalf, she came back out. Her hair, I noticed, was the same colour as the carpets and the upholstery on the chairs: the corporate colour. A shudder ran through me before I was able to rationally discount this as coincidence.

'Martin says he will be able to see you this time,' she said, with the same sadness, as if this was another let-down in a life of disappointments. 'Please take a seat in the interview room.'

Martin took another ten minutes to appear, not that I can talk, and inevitably looked no more than twenty-two years of age. He ran through an obviously much used routine about the bank and its products and then whipped out some paperwork that he said he'd read over with me, even if it was 'very simple'. I was still catching my breath at this point.

'What do you want the money for?' he asked. Computers, I told him, thinking briefly of Maggie. I had my half-truths at the ready, and we went through the usual motions, swapping them back and forth, with him doing all the writing as if I'd never learnt. He didn't look up once during the entire process, and after we'd finished I put my name on the dotted and he took it all with him to run through the system. It wasn't long before he was back.

'No,' he told me, 'I'm afraid not.' If I wanted to know why I had to write to a policy unit in Clacton-on-Sea. I'd been with them since I drew my first pay cheque and they were the only bank I'd ever had, but what else could you expect, a man like me? I took another look at myself in the mirrored wall on the way out, in my Merrywells shirt and tie, and told myself I had known what was coming next all along.

At the other end of Bedminster, down the alleyway that leads to the mail marketing building, was Selby and Co. They were the biggest loan sharks in town, or at least the biggest you could look up in a business directory, and before Bruce got me my job with McKellan the collection agency I worked for took bad debts off them for pennies to the pound. Buying paper, they call it. We all used to feel some scorn for the poor bastards stupid enough to borrow from Selby and Co.

They were tucked into the corner of an old paper mill, most of which was boarded up in my day, but it looked like someone had converted it into self-storage units now. I walked through the glass doors and waited in the lobby while the voice on the other side of the intercom assessed whether I was going to be a liability once inside the inner sanctum. They have had their problems, as you may imagine.

Inside, things had changed a bit. There were more people than I remembered, and most of them were wearing headsets and staring into computer screens. I didn't recognize anybody, and I wasn't surprised. I have no idea where they've gone, all the people I know.

'Can I help you?' asked a tall, dark-haired man who was doing a cheap impression of an eighties stockbroker. When I was a kid only clowns wore red braces, butchers and clowns.

'Yeah, I used to do business with Tony Carmel. Is he still here now?'

Alas, the last of the great moneylenders had been chased out of the temple. Bowel cancer, apparently. I'm sure that must have shagged up the seats of a few good suits. The bookkeeper hadn't changed, though, and I could see her at the same desk she'd always worked at.

'Kirsty!' I remembered, for some reason.

'Hi,' she said, baffled and embarrassed.

'Do you know this guy?' said the man in the red braces. Kirsty gave me a long look. There are times, these days, when I do not know whether it is best for me to be forgotten or remembered, which I would prefer. I always used to know. And I only changed my mind the once.

'Oh yeah,' she said, eventually, nodding. 'He was one of our debt collectors.'

'Right,' the man said, and strutted off, looking

busy and efficient, and who knows, maybe he was. Doubtless more so than me.

'We use a different agency now,' she said, in her hard Glaswegian. Maybe that was why I remembered her. 'They handle all that for us these days.'

'That's not why I'm here,' I said. 'I need a loan myself.'

For a brief moment you could see her wondering whether it was worth remonstrating with me, or whether I was already too far gone.

'Most of the loan applications come in over the phone now,' she said, hedging her bets, nodding in the direction of the headsetted rows.

'Seeing I'm here now anyway, isn't it possible to do it in person?'

'I suppose,' she said, finally writing me off. 'Go and tap one of those guys on the shoulder.'

'Can't I talk to someone who knows me? I mean, I have done a lot of business with you in the past.'

'I'll ask.'

I ended up talking to a red-haired bloke called Gerry. I never knew exactly what he did but he was important enough to have his own office these days.

Things were a lot more straightforward in here, if only because they never have to turn anybody away. They can raise the interest high enough to make anybody a worthwhile bet. Gerry pulled at his red beard, umming and ahhing in a farcical 'assessment' before trying to get me to borrow even more money. I refused. I know what the term sustainable debt means.

It was all going swimmingly until he reflected that I was an ex-debt-collector. There was me thinking this might have meant a better deal, being an old business associate and so on, but Gerry seemed to see it as an added risk. It meant I might be able to handle the people they sent out better than most, I suppose, but by that stage the debt's been sold, so what it's got to do with him I don't know. Nothing, in truth. It was just an excuse to up the rate once he'd established that the loan was potentially viable, once the light had appeared in my eyes. Never let them see you're hungry. It was too late for me. I argued my case, but I realized halfway through I was missing the point. I had already lost.

In the end I got five grand on thirty-five APR. If the job went to plan I could pay up within weeks and only suffer the early settlement penalty, about six hundred quid. They put the money through to my account on a CHAPS transfer that was supposedly instantaneous, and I walked out with the feeling that life had completed another full revolution.

By the time I was at my branch it was in. I withdrew five hundred over the counter from the lone cashier, who didn't bat an eyelid, and walked out in a state of shock. I hadn't been this flush before. Five hundred would cover the girl and a few beers, so seeing it was about lunchtime and I was in that neck of the woods I took the gamble of popping into the White Hart. Well, it was more a case of walking past and falling in rather than making any conscious decision, but it should be perfectly feasible, I thought, to spend less than two hours in there on a single visit. I'd feel better about that than the shininess of my bloody shoes, I can tell you. Lunch was shepherd's pie and jacket potato. The beer was John Smith's, draught, I should add, not smooth.

'Declan's looking for you,' said the landlord, in an ominous tone.

'Looking for me?' The attention of the little bugger could only herald bad tidings.

'You owe him money.'

Shit. I did. I owed him a hundred quid, but I had five hundred in my inside pocket and something almost mystical had happened to my bank account. The landlord watched my heart fall and rise out of my stomach. I thought of leaving the money behind the bar for him but it was asking for trouble.

People will go on about the inefficiency of the police force, for example, and then buy a twenty-grand sports car without a seventy-quid immobilizer. They'll leave their jacket on a park bench for ten minutes and be genuinely surprised to find it missing when they get back. They'll let an eight-year-old child out late at night on their own and then they'll cry bitterly for the rest of their lives. It doesn't take much, to be taken from.

'Yeah. I've been busy. Tell him I'll be in later tonight, if you see him,' I said.

'I will. I'll do that,' announced the landlord resolutely, and returned to contemplating the pint of Boddingtons he was pulling.

I borrowed the papers, although I don't think I read a word, and began on a few pints. It took a few to get me balanced after the morning's windfall. The initial disbelief mellowed into a mild and momentary euphoria, and then reality descended. If the job fell through, which was entirely possible, they'd pass me straight to the heavy mob. I knew all about that.

As strange as this may sound, given my intimacy with such surroundings, it became difficult to stay put. It was impossible not to see, with growing clarity, that I had only solved a problem with the introduction of a newer, bigger problem. All I could think about was the job, and the scope for fucking up was tremendous. It was already Thursday and I had no camera and no girl. There was no time for this.

I may even have left my drink unfinished when I crossed the road and joined the queue for the bus outside Asda, and the hydraulic doors had hissed open before I remembered I'd hired the Rover. I turned and headed off up to Greenways with barely a shrug of the shoulders: it has long ceased to surprise me, this kind of thing.

The car was still there, undamaged save for a long, serpentine scratch down the passenger side.

I thought it'd be OK outside Greenways, especially considering it's not the sort of motor you'd scratch out of spite. I'd forgotten about the number of kids around who must've grown tired of writing their names on letter boxes. Ah well, I thought, starting the engine. It was something for Mr Dinsdale to worry about. I had other concerns.

First I took the car around Lower Easton. It would be a lot cheaper if I could pick someone right off the street, and there's often a girl or two thereabouts by mid-afternoon, looking for a couple of quick tricks before the kids come back from school, or before other, less altruistic deadlines kick in, like withdrawal symptoms. The women who waited for buses that never came, as Bruce called them. There was one on the corner of Stapleton Road who had at least made some kind of effort. Her hair, which looked almost clean, was up in a tidy bunch and she was wearing a matching skirt and top, both of which fell firmly on the skimpy side of things.

I pulled up at the kerb and wound down my window. In seconds she had hobbled to my door.

'Hello,' was all she said. She had a smile that was all real but didn't sit well with what she was doing on Stapleton Road at half past two on a Thursday afternoon.

'You're high, aren't you?' I asked. 'You're on something.'

'Yeah.' She laughed, at my ignorance probably. 'I'm fucked.' It wasn't her stilettos which had slowed her approach to my car. She could hardly stand, and she had to slouch against the driver's door frame for support.

'Forget it. Bye,' I said, and then, when that didn't work: 'Look, you'll have to stand back. I'm going to drive off. The car will be moving. You'll fall over.'

That was all it took to remind me there was probably no budget option on this one. I left the car in the pay-and-display at the end of the M32, and there I was again: Old Market Street. Things that I have left behind have been brought around again. Beneath my feet, still steady this early in the day, under the paving slabs, I could sense the spinning of an invisible wheel. The old mistakes were lining up once more.

I headed for the ticket machine but I couldn't force myself to put any money in, despite all the cash in my wallet. If nobody came by I'd saved two or three bob; otherwise it was a hundred-and-fifty-quid fine. I don't know why it took me so long to realize I only went for the really long, point-less odds. Instead I took a lingering look up and down the street, trying to get a foothold, but these places can change overnight and the fronts said little.

You need to maintain a regular presence if you want to keep up with the market. The girls I needed were the good ones, and invariably they got out early and left no forwarding address. If I frequented these places I'd have names I could pull out of a hat, but I'd given up the vice personally and professionally. I'd made a special point of convincing myself that every entrapment was my last. Round about that moment, standing conspicuously on Old Market Street with a cigarette in a cupped hand, squinting unabashedly through the taffeta of a dozen open doorways, it became clear how stupid that was. I cannot really spare the time or money any more, between cases, to hide in the luxurious fiction that I will not do this work again. Maybe, I thought, I should face the music. It was already too late, far too late in life to pretend I didn't know who I was or what I did.

The first place I went to turned out to be fairly representative. Tinted windows hid a foyer with shag-pile carpets and an outdated three-piece suite, and in the corner was a reception desk made from artificial bamboo. The jungle motif appeared again on the walls and there were four girls in there, spread about the place like margarine, their limbs sedately akimbo on low-level furniture and bursting bean bags. There was no need to make an effort. It was only Thursday afternoon, and it was only me, the average punter. They eyed me indifferently and went back to their portable television.

More startling was the noise emanating from a nearby bedroom. An unseen headboard knocked against a nearby partition wall like a pneumatic hammer, somebody on a death-or-glory mission, a real orgasm-or-heart-attack job. It was impossible to ignore. The girls seemed to be ignoring it, or maybe they just didn't care, though it more than drowned out the sound of the telly.

'Hi,' said a short dumpy girl in a leather basque behind reception. She was probably about seventeen. I said nothing. The bed springs still screamed. 'Can we help you?'

'Yeah,' I said, conquering the blend of horror and lust I always get in these places. 'Maybe.'

Phrasing this might prove to be difficult.

'I'm looking for someone on behalf of a friend.'

She nodded with practised patience. She had heard this before. She had no idea that this time it was true, relatively speaking.

'Are you looking for someone or something in particular?' she asked over the mindless mechanical banging. There were no groans, no exclamations, no human noise at all, just the sound of the repetitive collisions produced when a certain kind of unstoppable force meets a particular type of immovable object. No one, nobody, ever gets what they want in these places. This is what I kept telling myself.

'Well,' I said, lighting a cigarette to numb the nerves, 'someone young, attractive – I mean genuinely attractive. With an education.' There was no point in being evasive. The girl stared at me blankly; I wasn't speaking her language. 'A redhead with big tits' was the sort of thing she could deal with.

'Will you know her when you see her?' she asked, taking the time to mark me down as a potentially dangerous freak.

'Probably.'

'Then have a look around,' she said, and sat down on her stool, reopening her magazine.

The girls were all attractive enough, all young. Other attributes were hard to ascertain. Like all professionals they kept certain things to themselves, and personality wasn't included in the price. It was hard to be objective, too, when for an insignificant dent in my brown envelope I could be doing something very subjective indeed. I didn't even know if I would ever be with another woman again, and outside these four walls was nothing but wind and rain and interest payments and a lonely death. I could forget all that, while it lasted, for less than the cost of a night in a good hotel. Not that much difference between the two, really, on one level: they're both refuges alluding to a permanence they cannot claim, and we are willing to believe them when we feel it is necessary.

'Hello,' I said. They took the trouble to look at me. 'The right girl can earn a lot of money for one night's work, straight sex, so could you just tell me a bit about yourselves?'

The girls were not ready for this, or they couldn't be arsed to reply, so the foyer remained silent save for the symphony of sex playing next door, a symphony in which the whole orchestra played the same note again and again for as long as it could stand.

'OK,' I said. 'Anyone studying at the moment? I know these are personal questions, I'm just working for someone with a bit of money. Please take the trouble to answer them because it makes things easier for all of us. So: anyone go to a girls' school? Anyone studying?'

'I'm in night school at the moment,' offered a black-haired girl with a pageboy haircut. Her accent wasn't too bad, but bad enough, and it was compounded by a slowness of speech that raised serious doubts about her general togetherness.

'Oh really?' I ventured. 'Studying what?'

'Health and beauty. I want to be a cosmetician.'

'Beautician, we used to call it,' I said, awkwardly. 'Well, that's good.' Nothing promising here. I decided to cut a long story short and get out:

'Listen, I'm just going to ask a couple of questions. If the answer to any of them is yes just say so, and don't lie, because I'll know. Any of you ever ride horses? And I don't mean donkeys on the beach at Weston-super-Mare.'

No answer.

'Anyone's dad wear a suit to work?'

Still no sound but the squeaking of bed springs.

'Anyone read books?'

Faces remained blank, but they were looking at me now. They were curious. If any of them were offended they didn't show it. When I turned round to talk to the dumpy girl in the basque she ducked her head down and pretended she'd been reading her magazine.

'When's the next shift on?' I asked, surprised at the volume of my own voice as the room fell suddenly silent for the first time. He was done, whoever he was. The unseen headboard was still once more with not even the humblest of grunts having passed.

'Six,' I think I heard her say.

There were four other places on Old Market Street, and every one was identical, though some were shabbier than others. The most promising candidate the daytime dainties offered was a little brown-haired girl studying A-levels at South Bristol College, but she was too young, young beyond her years and out of her depth. I'm sure she did a roaring trade but she was no seductress, unfortunately, and it was bad practice to place too many expectations on the husband.

The last place seemed almost wholesome in comparison to the rest of them. The girl behind the counter was practically my age, still borderline attractive in a dim light, and it looked like she'd been doing this for a while. She was the first person I'd met on that strange safari who called me 'love'. When I used to come here they called you little else, and it was something you said, rather than something you did, but at least it was mentioned. It made the whole thing feel a bit more natural. Nowadays it seems they don't call you anything at all, or worse they call you 'sir', in some misplaced attempt to convey a corporate air of professional service.

The woman smiled as soon as she saw me, like we were fellow survivors. I had the feeling we'd met before. She didn't seem to recognize me, but then I'd changed a bit since the days when I was hobnobbing with the regional crime squad and work was something more substantial than blackmail. I delivered a summons on a couple of occasions. Did criminal research for the prosecution in a murder case once. They'll hire you to do all sorts of things if they can trust you, and Bruce would always put a word in for me here and there. And everyone trusted McKellan. Oh, it wasn't bad, for a time. But now it was this.

'You've got two or three hours till the night girls come in,' she said. Close up I could see her face was slipping like molten plastic, folding in on itself like origami. It looked kind of friendly, all soft and mollifying. Too much time under the sun lamp, I suppose. She had dyed her hair beetroot red and it fell stiffly down to a bulging waistline, visible under a transparent bodice that showed everything right down to the hair around her nipples. It wasn't sexy, it was just honest. There was no other job she could have done, I'm sure. 'There's a nice pub just down the road, love, why don't you have a drink in there while you wait?'

It was a nice pub, the Boar's Head, all oak timbers and pewter tankards. About as genuine as apologies from a bailiff, of course, all bought wholesale from a warehouse somewhere and tacked on to a twentieth-century ceiling, but somebody somewhere was trying. Used to be a carpet shop, I think.

I started on the Guinness. It'd always seemed like a fortifying bit of booze to me, and I needed a dose of that right then. I hadn't wanted to come back here, I never did. My knees had been trembling on and off since I'd stepped into the first place, although they'd calmed by the time I'd had my chat with the faded madame in the willowy bodice. You do get used to it. That's the problem. I reached into my jacket for my fags and there were none there: I had been chain-smoking since I got out of the car.

The Boar's Head was relatively busy. It's a journalist's pub, and as such I imagine it's relatively busy most of the time, whenever it isn't busy outright or just closed. The police headquarters is sixty seconds away but they never came here, or they never used to. None were here now. Now there were only journalists from the *Evening Post* chucking back beer, together with a few quieter back-room types rolling cigarettes. I had another couple of pints, watching them for distraction's sake. It's not as if they were the sort who'd give you any aggravation if they caught you at it.

There's a full menu in the Boar's Head but right now I don't think I could handle a packet of peanuts. I know this, but I order chilli con carne and a jacket potato anyway, which I sit and watch go cold. I am not even kidding myself. Is this where all my money will go, I wonder? Will this be all?

Pints and pub lunches and pubescent sex: it wouldn't be that hard to piss and shit and fuck it all away. Nothing but immediate gratification of the lowest order, the most twisted and short-lived happiness you can get. I'd be buying myself nothing more than the usual lesson, except this time it'll be the last, because these kinds of lessons get harder as life goes on until it's too late, until the final fuck-up where the point of no return is reached and the only thing you learn is that you'll never know any better.

Then the lessons stop coming. They just become bitter reminders, the spiritual equivalent of being made to run fifty times around the playing fields after school, unpleasant and entirely uneducative. Coming out of the pub pissed at midday, last week's dinner on your shirt, throwing up in front of schoolchildren and even the prozzies laugh at you, even with all the money you throw at them. That sort of thing. I have embarked on similar spiralling descents, but at my age, in my condition, this one would be bottomless.

Fifteen thousand pounds could be squandered in six months with nothing in return but disgust, if you lived that long. Especially if you'd been conditioned by living hand to mouth for so much of your life, if getting by meant dropping everything to take what today offers, and for tomorrow nothing. There was no doubt about it, but then you've got to have more faith in yourself than that. You've got to at least give yourself the chances.

It was half six. Outside the pub work loomed, threateningly, as brooding as the sky. I had a brandy, then I had to go.

CHAPTER 2

Night was falling on Old Market Street. The shops and offices of the city centre pumped out their human effluvium. The wind was up and out they came, ties over shoulders, fringes in faces, blown around like litter. It broke through the insulation of the crowd and sent them staggering in their throngs, but they didn't mind one bit. It was the final exodus from the working day for the nine-to-fivers, and homes beckoned.

How safe they must feel, I thought. You wouldn't know to look at them that we were all just squatters in an oblivious city that was much too big to care about any of us. Groups divided and subdivided, individuals emerged, and an untold number of homeward journeys and evening adventures began. All of them were different, all of them unique, though in this part of town there was a common theme.

I watched some of them, finishing a cigarette in the doorway of the Boar's Head, buttoning my jacket. Sweating suits opened the doors of sex shops with trembling hands to stand in rooms full of shiny magazines and bright, direct lighting that was supposed to deter any funny business. The brothels would be filling up too, the mattresses getting warmer from the heat of successive bodies until the graveyard shift rolled around and only the weirdos came out. The squeaking of bed springs and banging of headboards was starting all over again. Tubes of lipstick and KY jelly were slowly and secretly emptying. It was all still here, for anyone who cared to look.

I visit the massage parlours in the same order. The faces have all changed, and the clientele is so densely packed now that I bump into other customers. Some are offended, many are threatened, others ignorant. A few are jovial, smiling, loving it: as if they'd found some kind of secret fraternity, some hidden brotherhood of man. Maybe some get what they pay for, I think. Maybe.

The girls are different but all the same and I will have to make a decision in the end. As the clock winds on, some innocuous leg-spreader will have this dubious honour conferred upon her. Mrs Dixon will baulk at first sight but I will tell her how it is. I will insist, and it will work out fine, as it has always done. Dixon will bite. In my experience most men will, especially if it's served up to them on a platter, clean and separate and removed. You've only got to create the moment. We all live in moments. Impulse is everything.

The second lap stretches out before me and by this stage the booze has taken the edge off it. I am confident enough, as I snake my way round the shag-piled bordellos and the dank velvety hallways that connect them to the outside world. My palms are hardly sweating at all.

I have nothing for these people now but scorn. It was all I ever had, but now I can believe it. Now there is less of the hypocrisy. I will never be here out of personal volition, outside company time, not any more. Now I am here on business only and these people are idiots. Maybe part of me has been saved after all, somewhere, because it doesn't interest me any more, this place. The mechanics all appear obvious now. You can smell them: cheap perfume over stale sweat and sex, like putting your jacket over the face of a corpse. Veins sunk deep by probing needles, bruises as black as tattoos, and poker eyes perennially unfazed by any of it, those alone saying more than any social worker's report ever could. The men are often a lot worse.

How many in one night, I wonder, for the average girl? Four or five hours of it, straight, no breaks? Are there queues, for the favourites? It was always different when I went. Kinder, almost. There was a tenderness about it. 'What'll it be, love?' they said, and I could still hear it, a faint and feeble echo of the past, something to juxtapose against the present: I am no longer part of Old Market Street. Having got the feel of the place for a second time I found it had become something other than what I wanted, or even needed, and for the most fleeting of moments it was almost uplifting. It had made me frightened of myself for too long.

There was a nervous, skinny lad, fresh out of his teens, pushing at the door of a sex shop when he should be pulling.

'The wind has a bit of a chill on it tonight, doesn't it?' I ask him. The lad stares at me as if I'd caught him masturbating. Luckily, he manages to let himself into the place before I have to tell him how. I almost laughed. The joke's on someone else for once, and it felt good being confident enough to take the piss.

I walked on that thin layer of conceit for about another ninety yards. That was all it took for the cold to cut through the booze and the wishful thinking to wear off. As self-deceptions go it was short lived, but it was up against huge odds. I am still here, after all, still buying sex, and I know full well that the woman picked will be the one I want most for myself. Critical distance is impossible. In fact, it's detrimental to the job.

Still no golden girl but there's a lot of dredging to be done. Four more brothels and the wandering street workers all lined up along Old Market Street like bottles on a wall, strutting the kerbs like tightrope walkers. I pass them all, on my tour, each and every visit as unpromising as the last, until I end up in the lobby with the fattening red-headed veteran.

'Hello again, love,' she says, remembering my face. 'A lot of them are busy at the moment. D'you want to sit down?'

I pick an armchair and dutch-fuck a fag, lighting up with the butt of my last before grinding it out on the rotting shag pile. It was getting very late in the day to come up with a willing seductress, and harder too to form any impression of the girls, who by now were, well, rushed off their feet. They didn't have the time to talk among themselves, let alone reply to questions they were naturally disinclined to answer in the first place. None of them looked like likely lasses but the situation was desperate, and I waited on in fading hope.

I wasn't the only man milling around the place, but I was milling more than most, and I drew some suspicious glances from those who came and went. I must have talked to thirty or forty girls that day, but it was one of the customers who told me I was on to something. I hadn't seen anything close, but I saw this guy leave the building and I knew she was there.

Six foot easy, beer-gutted, barrel-chested and tattooed like a Maori. Early to mid fifties, say. A labourer of some description: there was paint on his jeans and cement on his boots. Straight off the site, via a few quick ones at some nearby pub. Indulges in a bit of builder's banter with the girls, smiles unashamedly at the blokes. He hasn't been here before. He's here to see a girl the brickie went with last week.

I don't know how long he's in there for, nothing exceptional either way. When he emerges, head bowed, tucking in his grubby T-shirt as he beats his silent retreat, I just know. On the way in he was Jack the lad. On his way out he was a daft twat who was already too old for his job and had blown all his savings on prostitutes. It could have been anything, but I knew. They are not accustomed to doubt, these sorts of people.

She came out to the lobby shortly after and I pegged her straight away. Hair like honey and cheeks that glowed as if she'd just stepped into the changing rooms after the school lacrosse match. Her body was trim, but not slender. The first few years of adult excess had already begun to leave their mark, although I doubted they'd be allowed to have further effect.

'Hello, all,' she says, as if everybody was here for her alone. The accent was pure Radio 4. Some timid bloke is trying to mumble his interest but I walk over and hold her gaze.

'Are you next?' she asks, hands on hips, with the confidence of a prefect addressing an errant first-year.

'Kind of,' I reply. Dixon's a goner. 'Can I have a word in private?'

At the same time I hand her a business card, nothing special, just something that the machines in service stations will print out for two quid. I can't afford anything better, but it carries more weight than you might think. The words 'private investigator' impress more people than they should.

'Oh, righto,' she says, all smiles. She has found a bit of adventure. Undoubtedly, she is the right type of girl. She leads me into the first empty room off the corridor. If these places have lost the personal touch the accommodation has improved no end. I'd paid for worse in the Clifton hotel. The bed was made and seemingly unsoiled. There was a shower cubicle in the corner and crisp towels on the bedside table, along with bottles of shampoo and shower gel. When I went you got a bare mattress in a dark room, with piped music that was as out of place as a dinner suit in a dole queue. If it was supposed to stop the sounds travelling it didn't work.

'Go on then, Robin,' she said, cross-legged on the bed. She was wearing a flowery baby-doll dress and I could see almost all the way up to the jackpot. She was barefoot, but the soles of her feet looked as clean and soft as her face. The dress was all she was wearing and it was all she needed to wear.

'Well,' I say, drawing breath, 'I'm working on behalf of a client.'

'Oh yes?'

'Yeah. Would you be available for this line of work independent of the house? For one night only?'

'Rich or famous?'

'Sorry?'

'Who are you pimping for?' she asks, without malice. This will not be as exciting as she expects.

'It's not quite that simple.'

'It's just one person?' she interrupts. 'It's just one on one, yeah? With a man, I hope.'

'Absolutely. Listen, would you be available tonight to discuss this in the Hilton with me and my client?'

She isn't too sure. A suspicion that this isn't going to be quite what she imagined is already dawning.

'We'll pay for your time,' I say, knowing it won't be money wasted. 'Just for a chat, in a public place. Nothing sordid, just business. Speculative enquiries.'

'When, exactly?'

'A little after ten?'

'Fine,' she says, 'but I should warn you.' I could hear the cash till ring. 'I charge three hundred pounds an hour.'

She doesn't, and nor does anyone else on this street, but the fact she'd dare demand it is only proof of her aptitude, and I'm happy to leave the haggling till later. They don't have so much bargaining power after the act's actually been committed.

'No problem,' I reply. 'I'll pick you up at ten to.'

'Good-oh. See you later, then,' she says, unsmiling this time.

'Delia, isn't it?'

'Delia,' she repeated, and I walked out backwards like an idiot, feebly hiding the beginnings of an erection with my jacket. Outside, the lobby seemed lifeless. The girls out there looked like cardboard cut-outs, like drones. Like whores.

'Find what you want, did you, dearie?' The woman, the ageing siren with the flame-red hair and burnt-out body, beams.

'I think so.'

'Good,' she says. 'Everyone usually does, in here.'

'So it would seem,' I say, and we both grin, although hers looks a lot more authentic than mine. All part of the service, I'm sure, or it used to be.

Outside, the last traces of the working day had by now disappeared completely. The street was quiet and commuter free. People had got to wherever their roads took them when the clock struck five, and now there were only the punters and me. The people who would never get where they wanted, because their road was so long they'd never realize it just took them back to where they had been in one huge circle, like some treacherous desert track. It seemed so straight and simple, but without the landmarks, without the more significant things in life, it's impossible to notice the incline. It's beyond you to spot the almost invisible curvature that tells you you're walking in a gigantic, aimless loop.

But you're thirsty and the only thing you know how to do is keep going.

By the corner of Waterloo Street a marked Mondeo pulled out slow and quiet, like a shark swimming towards the shoal. Those easily spooked turned on their heels, heading for bus stops and newsagents', frightened, like minnows in its shadow. They're not what it's here for. No police force in the land is going to waste time trying to stop places like Old Market Street, not without some serious political pressure.

No, they were here for the pub by the printworks. It's always caused trouble. If it were a free house then it wouldn't be a problem, the owner would learn to handle his territory or sell out, but the pubco shipped in some young couple almost every other month. None ever had any experience, otherwise they'd have gone somewhere else. I think they were drawn by the offer of a free flat above the pub. It certainly wasn't the money. Understandably, with management like that the clientele know they can take advantage, and they do. Someone used to get called out a couple of times a week when I drank around here. There's violence, always, and it tends to be the same people.

The big bland Mondeo beaches itself on the kerb outside the pub and slows to a standstill by the doors. The two young guys inside, both uniformed, can't be past their early twenties. I can tell they're sharp. Any policeman that looks it usually is.

I came to a standstill myself, captivated, on the opposite side of the road. Out of the car, easy and casual. Leave the caps on the seats: they'll only get in the way. Truncheons loose and ready at the waist. They've been doing this for a year or two now and they're confident because they know they're good at it. They won't be on the beat much longer. One brushes something off his jumper while the other holds the front door open for him. Then he unclips his truncheon from his belt, only it's a nightstick these days, and pushes the second inside door open, peering around it. The pub goes quiet. Then they're both in, the doors falling shut behind them.

It'll only take a minute, I think, leaning back against the cool glass window of an empty shop. The punters pretending to be waiting for a bus relax, now they know they're not on the wanted list, and head off to cash in their lust.

The pub was called the Eagle. In my day it was the Rose and Crown. It's been called a lot of things since then, but everything's as it's always been, and will continue so. Inside, the bobbies do their business, and there's nothing on the outside to suggest the probable smashing of glasses and faces save the silent revolving lights of the patrol car, casting its coloured beams up and down Old Market Street. I wonder whether I could ever have been as natural as either of those two, straight in, truncheon first, with crisp creases in their shirtsleeves.

The doors open again, suddenly this time, slamming against the walls, and a ginger-haired man in a ripped Reebok sweatshirt and hand-cuffs emerges, propelled by the two coppers, a drunken man concussed into submission. When they slide him into the back seat his head hangs so low you'd think his neck was broken. Seconds ago he was brandishing an empty bottle and raging like a hurricane about fuck-all, now he's found himself thrown into the back of a police Mondeo like a sack of potatoes. It can't be the first time.

As if it is something of an afterthought, which it isn't, one of them turns back into the pub to administer a few words along the usual lines. Then they put their hats back on and drive off, with the blue lights flashing noiselessly as they go. Their whole careers ahead of them, and they are bright, hard and indestructible.

The street seems far quieter now than it was before. A black girl hustles for business four or five steps away with nothing more than a raised eyebrow and a curled lip. I catch a glimpse of myself in the shop window and realize that we are all ghosts here. I am as ethereal as everyone else on this street. We can touch nothing, nor will any of us leave any trace of our passing. Something has been shut off to us, I think, looking at the people around me, each one a little bit hungrier when they leave than when they went in. Lost, utterly. No one with a single landmark to go by.

For a long time I really did think that things would have been different, if only they'd let me join the force.

Eyesight, they said. It was just starting to go then. Didn't even know about it myself. They said it was possible it would pick up in a year or two, but of course it didn't, and I would have had trouble passing the physical by then anyway. I have always been a drinking man. You don't notice at the start, because you can account for your early years as youthful indulgence, and even after that you need a few more years again before things accumulate enough to be noticeable, especially if it comes in fits and starts.

I made my application when I was starting out, working for an insurance firm in the centre of town, although I wince to remember it. You have to go through a lot of closed doors to go back that far, you have to cross a gaping chasm of wasted opportunities. I think I held my end up there for about two and a half years, and I had a second and a third, maybe a fourth, chance in some other places, and then, it seemed, I didn't have any chances left. Then came the donkey work. Shit, I was in double glazing for a few years. Then I wound up debt collecting, and when you're doing that it doesn't matter what time you get out of bed or what your breath smells like, as long as you come back with something. It was all right for a while, like I said, before the area manager started coming on like some latter-day Sheriff of

Nottingham. So when Bruce offered me the position with McKellan it was almost an old dream come true. For a time.

I wonder what they really thought of me, Bruce and Knight and Gilboursen and the rest. I don't remember telling them about my failed attempt to join the thin blue line but then you say a lot of stuff when you're three sheets to the wind. It must have been obvious enough. I think they respected me, though, or came to. This is how I explain the silence, the cut-off: you can't fall out with somebody you've already written off.

That said, I still didn't know why exactly they cut me off in the first place. I didn't know whether it was because I grassed or because I'd done something to grass about. The way some of them acted you'd think they were as pure as the driven snow, and I was willing to believe that then, but nevertheless in my position there was nothing else I could have done but take and then tell. I couldn't have turned away the boys who were after him any more than I could have turned away Bruce in the first place. It is important to maintain good relations all round, you know, when you're self-employed, and whatever I spilled surely wasn't enough to build a prosecution on. Nobody will know now, now that Bruce got spread over half of Royal Oak Avenue before anyone could try, and the only certainty I had was that whatever they really were, I couldn't call them friends any more.

I am drunk when I get back to the car. I can tell from the time it takes to unlock the door, the key skating over the bodywork as if I am etching the bloody thing. And I'm exhausted. I pull the safety belt across me and it feels like it weighs about sixty pounds. I start the car in gear and it kangaroos into a stall. I restart the engine, out of gear now, and after a few screaming yards notice I've left the handbrake on.

Motion is attained eventually. I'm too tired and too pissed for this, I think, swinging the car round the one-way lanes of the car park so many times I feel lost before I reach the road. But I am always too tired or too pissed, neither had ever been any kind of excuse, and I would drive if I had to. This was nothing new. It was just that the next time they stopped me it'd be a ban for life, or community service, or prison. That'd be the end of it all then, and what little there was left to me would finally fall away and I'd move the small distance necessary for me to plummet into complete ruin. There was a sick child in me that wanted it to happen, I swear.

Then I was shooting down the double barrels of the carriageway like a swimmer breaking for the surface, outrunning the undertow of Old Market Street with my foot to the floor, and it wasn't fast enough. The feelings it had awakened rolled after me like clouds, after the place itself was half a city behind me.

I had about a hundred and fifty minutes before

141

the next ordeal of the evening, and as I sideswiped a roundabout with the gentlest of curves I decided impulsively that I'd get as far away as I could. I needed breathing space and thinking time so badly I was doing over ninety before I'd left the city centre, and I broke the ton on the centre line where the big left-hander cut into Bond Street. I can still remember calmly watching the car swerve in and out of the lanes after I'd touched the brakes, wondering in that compressed, gliding moment whether I'd left traction for the last time, but the skid swelled and fell away like a wave, and I felt the wheels return to the control of my shivering palms.

By Temple Meads I was breathing hard, hugging thirty and trembling with restraint, following the hill up to my flat like a homing pigeon, stuck in an old and unwelcome groove, remembering about my token escape, my doomed sally, just in time to shift two gears lower and with a heavy heel slip more or less unscathed, screeching and two-wheeled, through the honking traffic into the lane for Bath Road and beyond, a messy slew of cars in my wake as I disappeared down the junction. Why I felt these risks were justified I couldn't say, but I felt it, right down to my trembling toes, light as sparrows on the pedals.

I kept it up this time, too scared to let the flushed, firing cylinders dim until I could see with my own eyes the city changing shape. By then I was venturing into the out-of-town shopping centres and industrial estates, the cineplexes and the drive-thrus, and as the dense streets grew sparser, I let her cruise.

Here the suburbs began anew, the outer rim of houses once separate settlements in their own right, and the road rolled uphill so gradually I almost didn't notice it until the descent on the other side, where the city shrank away, and on my right the countryside began. I was somewhere out towards Keynsham, on the county border. The back gardens of the latest housing estate looked wistfully out over the road at the un-developed space beyond. This was the front line between Bristol and the half-hearted green belt, not so much fields and farms as golf courses and nursing homes, at least for now. The high-water mark is miles away yet, if it ever stops expanding at all.

I chanced it for half a mile, pressing on, wondering what I thought I was doing. Then, out there in the hinterlands of a hinterland city, there appeared by the roadside a forlorn and blatantly unprofitable pub called the Traveller's Rest. The car park was empty except for a battered Volvo estate. It wasn't much but it was far enough, and five hundred yards away you could see the last lamplit strands of the city finally surrendering the land to the docile flocks and munching herds.

I'm the only customer. The barman has to be the landlord, not only because such a venture obviously can't afford staff but because in his friendliness lies the desperation of a man who is going steadily bust on a losing game.

'Come far?' he asks.

'No. Not at all.' Not far enough.

His wife even comes down to talk to me, like some lonely widow whose family never visits. It is not a happy place. They pass some observations about the local housing estate and the price of petrol which both fall on deaf ears.

'Do you have the paper?' I ask, pre-empting another doomed conversational gambit.

'No, sorry,' says the barman, understanding he has blown it again. 'Do you want to watch the telly?'

'Please.'

They are common enough, these dying pubs on the fringes of the city. The men who swallowed six pints after each day's work are gone, and their sons and grandsons eke out what succour they need from the boxes of wine on their fridge-tops. We are a dying breed, us unabashed boozers.

Outside, under a faint halogen light, there was a children's playground, doubtless a frantic bid to attract family custom, but it had been a wasted investment. The swings and slides and climbing frames in their bright colouring-book shades couldn't have been a year old, but the place looked spookier than a cemetery, and equally lifeless. Inside, the barman was resigned once more to silence, and the telly told its daily tale of atrocity.

I'm not really watching. I have covered maybe four or five miles; further out than I've been in some time. As far as I've been in years, and here I am, drinking stale bitter and staring at a screen I do not want to see, scared of making eye contact, just because we both know that he is going under, and cannot say so. There is nothing more for me out here. The boundaries of my life have become clearly marked.

I declined another pint and got out before the place burnt down in a pre-arranged fire. Maybe in an hour or two I could really let go, and drink myself out of it. I took the drive back as slowly as I could but even then I found myself outside the sauna ten minutes too soon, waiting kerb-side in the Rover, making the punters feel uneasy. I have been jittery all day and I am still nervous now. Too close, I think, I am too close by far.

She sticks her head out at quarter past. I flash my lights and she comes running to the passenger side. The short dress has been tucked into a pair of blue jeans and her bare feet are encased in Doc Martens. She still looks fresh, even after her shift, and I assume she showered before she left, probably more than once. How often do you have to clean yourself, I wonder, doing a job like that?

She shuts the car door gently behind her and I pull out. Over the gentle hum of the fan heaters I can hear her body nestling quietly on the seat next to mine.

'It shouldn't take long,' I say. I have to say something.

'I know,' she says. The denim is skin tight, sprayed on. I can trace the line of her fine legs right up from the ankles, up to where-I-know-better.

'So, how old are you, Delia?'

'Twenty-one.' Perfect.

'Are you at university?'

'Why do you ask?'

'Well, I was wondering. Your background is a factor, you see.'

'I shouldn't think you'd have to worry about that,' she said, with a well-pronounced emphasis. Where does it come from, all this confidence? And where does it go? I was just the same, at her age. 'What sort of person are you after, anyway?'

'Well, why don't you talk to my client about that?' If Mrs Dixon wanted to meet the girl then she could do the talking: no point in making more work for myself. For the rest of the journey we said nothing, and I listened to her leather jacket squeak against the seat whenever she moved her body.

The Hilton had a basement car park and an attendant who was actually wearing a top hat. In a spotless performance he waved us through as if we were as important as everybody else, and I put the car to rest between its vehicular superiors.

We got out and went through the double doors

in the near wall. The diesel-stained concrete turned to wine-coloured carpet in a flash and I heaved my lumbering body up the two flights of Axminster steps it took to reach ground level. Delia's sprightly figure bounced patiently alongside me. She still had a lot of energy, even after her shift.

'So, what's he like, then, this client?' she asked, curiosity finally getting the better of her as we entered the lobby.

'He's a she, for starters,' I said between breaths as I looked around for the bar, hoping there'd only be one in the building. There was. It was a long, dark-wood-panelled job that stretched along the front of the hotel. The windows were tinted and you'd never notice it from the outside.

'I don't know about that, Robin,' she said, mock flustered. 'That changes things a little. I really don't know about that at all.'

'It's not like that,' I said. 'Don't worry.' Delia wasn't worried at all, just miffed she'd lost the chance to up her fee. It would come.

Like I say, the bar was pretty discreet. Just a few businessmen and women dotted around the place, most of whom probably couldn't speak English anyway. It was a good call. I was surprised, then, to find she wasn't there. Few people in life are later than I, and it usually means something is wrong. I did a few circuits, probably not very subtly, and for no other reason than I didn't know what to do. Delia must have felt a smidgen of

147

suspense every time I passed somebody but she didn't show it.

'She's not here. Yet,' I concluded, unnecessarily, the two of us standing back in the bar's entrance where I had seen at first glance this was so. Delia nodded, and then I was silent under the weight of the impending conversation I would now have to conduct unsupported. Relatively speaking.

'I'm going to have a drink,' I said, leaving it open. It didn't seem quite right to offer. She followed anyway.

I had a Heineken, a fairly innocuous lager, and she bolted on an order for a Manhattan on her own initiative. I didn't know what a Manhattan was, and still don't, but it didn't look out of place. I was on the verge of saying something about the quality of the service, or how the nights had drawn in, when a balding man in a waistcoat announced rather formally that there was a call for a Mr Lou-Ellen. I didn't know exactly what I could say without Mrs Dixon's seal of approval, so I was fairly relieved. You have to say something to a girl like that, or at least you do if you're a middle-aged man of indeterminate attractiveness who has lived alone for the past twenty years. The phone was in a row of booths delicately placed out of reception's earshot.

'Running late?' I asked, picking up the receiver left dangling like a hanged man.

'I can't make it, I'm afraid.'

'What do you want to do?'

148

'Put her on. I'll have to speak to her over the phone. Don't worry, I won't tell her anything about the job.'

I asked her whether she was sure, and of course she was, so then I waved Delia in from the hall so nobody would hang up on my client.

'She isn't able to make it tonight,' I explained. 'But she wants to talk to you. Over there.'

I pointed her in the right direction and went to rescue my pint before some over-zealous barman poured it into the slop tray. A table emptied near by and I took it, territorially slapping my cigarettes down on its surface. The bar got busier but nobody joined me, and there were three empty seats. I took it as a snub but was grateful regardless. Delia was on the phone for twenty minutes or so, although it could have been less. She had probably been waving at me for some time before I noticed her, busy as I was with the business end of another lager. She winked at me as I passed and I took this to mean she'd passed the audition.

'What exactly did you tell that girl?' I asked, the earpiece still warm from her body.

'Oh, hardly anything,' Mrs Dixon answered. 'Only the vaguest of details. She'll do.'

'I told you,' I said, but felt no smugness.

'You'd better get that room booked. It'll be pretty packed on Saturday with the conference.'

'Understood.'

'Book it from tonight, if you like.'

'I'm not sure that's an absolutely necessary expense.'

'Well, put it on the bill, if you must. Two rooms, if you need them. I think you said something about two rooms, didn't you? Just don't worry, OK?'

'We'll see,' I said, wondering where this sudden pleasantness was coming from. Desperation, I assumed, from a greedy woman in a hurry. 'I'd better go and discuss terms with our friend.' Then I hung up, before she told me not to worry a third time, or asked me how I was.

Delia had found my table and was sitting there with another round of drinks for us both. She looked a lot younger, in that huge leather armchair. I sat down and lit up a cigarette, draining a third or so of my pint while I thought of what to say and in what order to say it. Delia didn't say anything either. Perhaps she had the same problem. I rubbed my forehead; a hangover had started to come on but it could be outdrunk.

'How long have you been doing this?' I asked. I could just talk around it for now. It was all I was up to.

'Long enough,' she said quickly, putting on a bold smile, which I took to mean not very long at all. Not that experience really mattered. 'How long have you been doing it?'

'Oh, long enough,' I said, trying to smile and possibly succeeding. I offered her a fag but she took out her own ultra-low-tar something or other. 'Believe me.'

I watched her smoke, just to see whether she could do it properly, but she wasn't that young.

'Maybe it doesn't matter,' I thought, or thought I thought. 'Maybe you only have to do it once and that's all it takes.' She had to ask me twice what I was talking about before I snapped back, shifting my focus from the hazy middle distance to her engaging expression. Then I knew I had said it aloud, that an anchor was slipping, the drink or her youth, her beauty, I don't know why. Never mind, I was going to say, but it seemed to take its time coming out.

'In that case maybe it doesn't matter at all,' she said in the interim, understanding. 'You're just that sort of person, you know, and you don't know about it. You just haven't done it. What's the difference?'

'I don't know,' I said, and I really didn't have a fucking clue. Philosophy was outside my grasp at the time, as it always is whenever I feel compelled to talk about it. 'Why do you do it, what you do?'

'I had a kid.'

'Oh,' I said, oh, and crawled off to the bar like pond scum, skating off the same question before she could ask it of me. I downed a dark rum there while they mixed her cocktail and came back with the same drinks.

'So, the job,' I said. 'Tell me exactly what you know about it. I don't want to repeat myself.'

'There's a man coming here Saturday night and I'm going to take him to bed.'

151

'That's fine,' I said, although to be honest I'd have preferred it if she hadn't known anything at all. 'He's been having a bad time of it recently, you know, and he needs to relax. So this is going to be a nice surprise for him. It's just he's very clean cut, very straight laced, and if he knew you were a working girl he'd probably steer clear. So don't mention it. In fact, keep it under wraps. He needs the flattery'. This all came out very easily. It probably wasn't very convincing but I was pissed, and it just rolled off. I was even aware of it at the time but it didn't bother me; I spout all kinds of shit when drinking and it had rarely bothered me before. I knew this girl was only going to ask the pertinent questions. I was the blabber.

'If he turns me down do I still get paid?'

'No.'

'I don't need to waste my time like that. I can make guaranteed money working where you found me.'

'OK,' I said. I was being a tad unrealistic. 'How much do you think, just for showing up?'

'I want four hundred no matter what happens. If I sleep with him I want another six.'

'A grand?' It was too much.

'This isn't a straightforward lay.'

Nobody could expect a thousand. A grand was too much. If you had a kid it probably wasn't. She had a kid. Most of them must have had kids, it occurred to me, they didn't look like junkies. I puffed on my fag, drank my weak lager, stroked my chin, looked thoughtful and failed utterly to convince myself it was worth the bother.

'OK. I'll give you two hundred up front and eight hundred if you do the job that's been asked of you,' I said. I had to give her some kind of incentive. It was the quickest deal I'd ever struck, and I think I had every intention of honouring it too.

She nodded and leant back in her chair, taming a wisp of stray hair behind her ear, saying something I couldn't follow. I was trying to balance the books but my head was in that numb wasteland between hangover and alcoholic freefall and I couldn't remember all the numbers. They didn't look too good, anyway.

'A grand's too much,' I said, again. Delia kept talking.

'We can sort it out,' she was saying. I noticed that my glass was empty so I got up on autopilot to go to the bar, time to start on the shorts now maybe, but somehow I was out in reception looking at a woman my age in a maroon blouse with gold buttons, shrivelled thin with night shifts and missed dinners, the air around her thick with hairspray. It smelt like vodka. 'We can sort it out.'

I booked a room from that night up till Saturday, thinking there might be some problems because of the conference, but nobody said anything, they only asked me for my luggage and I didn't have any, and the woman started staring over my shoulder in a sordid, disapproving sort of way, and

I turned and she was standing smiling there behind me, this young pretty mother about twenty years of age, and she took my hand, she held my bloody hand as I recall, all the way up the stairs.

CHAPTER 3

When day came, and it came early as it always does on these mornings, when my eyelids broke free from their film of sleep to see the pale glow on the other side of the curtains, I swear it made a noise like the crack of rifle fire. As if a combat zone had crept up on me in the night, which it had, in a way. I almost wanted to take cover behind the bed but it was a good, clean shot and only one was needed. I got it right in the heart, and felt my life ebb away as the memory flooded in, but I couldn't die.

I could only stay in bed and turn my face away from the light, while my guts, shot to hell, ached their queasy complaint. A novice would have tried to absolve himself bent-headed over the toilet bowl, but that just weakens you more. You have to keep it down, hold it in, and endure; you have to keep a lid on it until it fades away ignored. I could see the space where she had lain. That was all it was, a space. It was there before and it was there after.

Oh, she was beautiful. She may have been the most beautiful, it was hard to say, time treats some women differently and even I was in love once. I don't know whether it counts for anything; it wasn't her beauty she played on. All I wanted was to hold her. That was all I wanted, at first.

She put a lot of effort into it. Had to, the state I was in, and she succeeded. Then the beauty became elusive, through the groaning and the grimacing and empty sighs, and no less lurid than the printed pink of a dirty magazine, and you could only see it through half-closed eyes in the right frame of mind. Most of the time my frame of mind was all wrong, or I was looking too closely. It wasn't difficult: she'd left the lights on for effect, and on the rare occasions when our eyes actually met there was only an awkwardness she hid with a glaze, quite professional, which made her seem like she was in another room. Like her body was something anonymous instead of close and real enough for me to feel the soft down on her tender rear, or stroke the stretch marks on her hips, sense the sad and strangely steady beat of her heart. I wondered how old her kid was, was it a boy or a girl, who the father was, and then the room began to ripple and contract and for a while I wondered nothing at all.

I spent my seed. Inevitably. The levers were all pushed, gears engaged, circuits activated correctly. I was grateful she had the decency not to pretend to come herself. Every man prefers the lie, I know better than most, but it would have been a lie too far. Our little conceit would have collapsed in on us entirely. There was a respite, I don't know how long, in which nothing was said. Lovers would have fallen upon each other, resting and gazing. She collected herself on the far side of the bed. I didn't know where to look; even the ceiling seemed implicated.

The silence grew to a noticeable level, and I wondered what it was there for, trying very hard not to think there was a possibility she was waiting for attention or conversation. I knew she wasn't. Then I understood and gave her the two hundred I'd told her I would. She put it in a little clasp purse in her shoulder bag and asked me, standing erect in the buff, pert and complete, whether she could have some money for the taxi. It didn't seem worth making a fuss about.

'Well, see you, then,' she'd said, picking up her clothes.

'See you?'

'Lectures in the morning. University.'

I watched her tuck her dress back into her jeans and buckle her belt. She applied a little lipstick in the mirror above the desk, pouted at her reflection, and buttoned her jacket. I grasped for words; I trawled the past in desperation for things I hadn't said in decades. She was already at the door.

'What do you study?' I asked, too late, to the sound of its closing. There was no hiding anything now, no longer any possibility of a better pretence, of a shade of intimacy with which to draw a veil over the act. Now I was left alone, with the knowledge that I'd been given an opportunity to prove something to myself and that I had failed. Expectantly I eyed the lines of my ageing body, the crumples in the sheets, the humming glow of the minibar, but it was from the shadowy corners of the room that the depression rose. You're gonna die alone, it sang, you fucker. I switched on the telly, turning it up to a volume that should have brought angry thumping on the walls, and opened the tiny fridge.

I don't want any of this, I thought, I want nothing to do with it. It was the second time I'd felt that way in as many days. It is not good for me, this type of work. The money is the key. Try to believe it, I thought, collecting the miniature spirit bottles and lining them up on the window sill. The power to steer the ship towards the shore. I pulled a chair up alongside them and unscrewed the first. Behind me Rommel had taken Tobruk in grainy black and white.

Outside, the city lived on, the stray taxi hurtling by like a pulse down a vein. The snoring man on the bench, the unconscious woman in the doorway, the lonely silhouette on the bridge, the soft-footed copper treading the empty street like a minefield: it was not unaware, it saw it all and never looked away. For all the booze inside me, for all my desperation, I could only hold its gaze for an hour before I had to shift away and let the curtains fall, an interval in an unwritten perform- ance with no opening act and no scripted end.

I've never been one for long, dark nights of the soul. I've tried, but I just couldn't stay awake. When my eyelids shuddered shut it was to late-night repeats of the previous year's Formula One season. There is an appropriate metaphor here for something, I thought, though I wasn't sure what. It was clear something was mirrored in this hugely expensive, wasteful sport, watching the cars hurtle round the same track ad infinitum, the chicanes and sweeping curves tracing a secret and obscure cipher. I remembered hearing somewhere that if an untrained driver put his foot to the floor in those things the acceleration would break his neck. But they said that about Stephenson's *Rocket*, didn't they, and then sleep must have come but I don't remember that at all. Only that crack like rifle fire. God knows where that came from, telling me that everything I was hiding from had moved a day closer, was out there, in the cold ashen dawn behind the curtains.

I sat up to find I had spilt whisky over my clothes. There were still some clear spirits on the sill, some vodka or gin, so I had gone down fighting. I'd still lost. Time had stolen round in the middle of the night and deposited another day at my feet while no one was looking. It had seeped in through the crack under the door, surrounded the ranch like Red Indians. It wailed up at me triumphantly from the street like a spoilt child: you cannot stop these things.

That night was the set-up; secret cameras and

hidden mikes. The following night was the seduction. The night after: the money, and mornings as fucked up as this for the foreseeable future, which was for ever. I put my clothes on the radiator and had a shower, waiting in the steam until all that was left of the previous night's transgressions had drained away. All that you could get down a plughole.

I stepped out of the shower as clean as a newborn babe, and put on clothes as filthy as a car-crash tourniquet. It makes you wonder what the point of it all is. The dividing line between mere problems of personal hygiene and the attention of the social services, I suppose. I wet my hair and let it fall back on my scalp. My hairline had inched upwards again in the last few days, I was sure of it. Underneath its stealthy advance my brain rang like a monastery bell, a constant, rhythmic litany of pain, and each step on the stairway down felt like an alpine descent. I saw myself tumbling like a sot, cast for all to see into some shameful pit by a sober god, but somehow I kept my balance.

What next? Breakfast was as good an idea as any other. I wasn't hungry but it was a free meal and ergo I was having it: we all have our ways of keeping ourselves in check, like those tuxedoed Victorian explorers in the wilderness, making a point of passing the port to the left under the jungle canopy. They would, I think, have understood what this was about. The hotel restaurant was almost entirely pink, apart from some white colonial latticework and a generous over-helping of fake flora, which, while not looking particularly realistic, really was as densely abundant as jungle in places. At first glance I thought I might be hallucinating; it was like the Jockey Club meets Barbara Cartland, and there were no windows. It was designed, I think, to ensure that guests such as myself spent as little time there as possible, and in this it was entirely successful.

I found a spot where the plastic ivy wouldn't dangle into my cereal and managed a few spoonfuls of sugary, soggy something or other. Again, the place was almost empty. It was just me and the usual handful of suits that had passed for company recently; mostly a male affair, although there were a few powerful-looking skirts around. They sat at tables of one, browsing through the quality broadsheets, answering mobile phones, writing things in leather Filofaxes. I was free to focus my thoughts on my own business, and like I said, I was out of there as soon as possible.

'Morning, sir,' said a different doorman, although I wouldn't be surprised if the top hat was the same. My car was still there, abandoned by the luxury saloons that had by now glided off to their various appointments. I tuned into a local radio station, lit up a fag, and cruised out. Right into the morning traffic, set on the road like concrete.

They revved like stock cars at the starting line, but no green light would come. The only things moving here were the rising plumes of hot exhaust. God knows how long it would have taken to get into St Pauls, even assuming someone had retained enough humanity to let me out. I reversed back into the parking space, opting to amble about on my own two untrustworthy legs until the roads had cleared.

I marched out briskly in the direction of the docks. It wasn't warm enough for a slower pace, and the other direction led back up to Totterdown. It had been my intention to use the time to organize my day, but walking has never really been about thinking for me, more the opposite. Things to do today – I ticked them off mentally: buy surveillance equipment, fit surveillance equipment, and oh, sort out that bloody locksmith if at all possible. That was as much as I covered before reaching St Mary Redcliffe's, and then I forgot all about it.

For all the stick the Christian set gets, however small the dwindling flock, they have something. Not all of us believe we can be saved: don't knock it. I had my share of it when I was a boy. It's all rubbed off now, though, like the tooth fairy and Father Christmas, but they laid it on. Whether the gossiping pews were quiet now, whether the dirge-like hymns still rolled down the hillsides like boulders, I couldn't say. I couldn't see that kind of solidarity anywhere any more, except perhaps in the force, and that was denied to me. So, no, you wouldn't catch me in there, marriages and funerals only, I'm afraid, and I don't see any invitations for either of those coming my way. It didn't stop me strolling under the buttresses, or craning my neck at the spire. I even stood in the doorway, gazing into the gloom, but there is always something kind of sad to me about empty churches. The smell, maybe, or the handwritten signs begging quietly for spare change, a new roof, more believers. The rows of frayed and forlorn hymn books whose pages must be rotting together. It's probably worse when there's a service on.

So I passed St Mary's by and then I was over the swing bridge and down into the docks, a graveyard of a different kind. Powerboats bobbed pompously where merchant ships once moored. The storehouses were tenantless flats, still swapped around by property dealers like they were gold dust. Only the seagulls remember.

There's a species of seagull that can live for up to a hundred years, I forget which one. It wasn't too improbable that one or two of the big birds flapping about the place on wizened feathers knew it when it was something else entirely, when the cobblestones were more than just parking spaces for cars with walnut dashes. Not that I'm getting nostalgic. Things do change; just too much or not enough.

I strolled on a bit, looking for something that I couldn't name and wasn't there, and ended up sitting on the pedestal of the John Cabot statue, smoking a cigarette while John maintained his vigil over the cold, lapping water. Cabot was a local lad who discovered America, at least according to the city council. It's not what I was taught at school, but then there were many things they never mentioned. Cabot too has his own lessons to learn. The world is smaller these days, and now he gazes out at nothing more than the AA call centre and a park-and-ride. An unwitting sculptor and a clutch of indifferent developers have rendered him a village idiot. The old long, open vistas have all closed in on themselves, and so have we, I think, walking back to the hotel after another morning smoke, staring down at the city afloat in the water. I know these streets too well to know them at all.

On the walk back to the hotel every cracked slab of paving held the face of a person I'd met once before but couldn't remember. The steady, shifting colours of the traffic lights, the faded fly posters clinging to the corrugated iron, the way the litter blew around the over-brimming bins, the sloping illiterate scrawl of the small ads in the newsagents' windows, somewhere in all these things hid runes I could no longer read, whose message I had misplaced over time. Somehow I had become a stranger again.

I stopped at the hole in the wall and took out five hundred, which seemed to have become the float for this job. I was going through it pretty quickly so I decided to get a quote for the recording equipment as soon as possible. When I got to the Hilton I went straight down the ramp to the car park, and the top-hatted doorman, too well trained to think, too conditioned to consider, still waved me through, although you could tell he was unsure of the protocol for greeting whisky-stained pedestrians.

Now that the flash flood of rush-hour traffic had subsided the roads were clear again. It was all part of the city's schizophrenia that these streets were either drowning with people or as empty as canyons. Their status switched more quickly than slides in a projector, so sudden it was surreal. Turning your back on it for ten minutes was all that was necessary, or taking a new turning; walking ninety random yards. The bleating of the crowd would defer to the empty echoes of your footsteps and back again, twin cities in the same place.

I knew which one I belonged to, and when I got the Rover out I knew too I would be able to drive as the planners had intended. Within minutes I'd left the hotel behind, and I was entering a place that they still hadn't managed to eradicate. St Pauls hasn't changed much over the years. The money is still staying away. It's always the poor parts of town which grant the city its continuity; poverty cannot afford to change too much. The shards of broken bottles still line the tops of the breeze-block walls.

I know St Pauls well. They had me running round here like a headless chicken at one time. The only valuables people seem to legally come by in this part of town are on the never-never, and when the never-never became legal fees and final demands it was usually in St Pauls. The vans came and went like ambulances. There were doorstep scenes here every day.

I remember once I had to pick up some furniture, me and one of the boys, and we stopped outside this terrace and I went a-knocking. This woman opened the door, early twenties, a kid in her arms and a few more raising havoc in the background, and that was her first mistake, because once you open a door to a debt collector they're in. She started panicking, a woman in the house on her own with this strange and very physical man, so I waved my piece of paper at her and she seemed to calm down once she knew she wasn't going to get raped over the kitchen sideboard.

Except there was no kitchen sideboard. I swear, the only furniture in the whole house was this spanking-new full-leather three-piece and matching recliner. Some commission-hungry salesman had let it slip the credit net. I didn't go upstairs, so I don't know about that, but she did offer. I'd heard stories about it before but it had never happened to me. At first I thought, I'm not such a bad-looking bloke, maybe it's just like having it off with the milkman. Then her voice started to crack and the kids seemed to be everywhere and it was the only fucking furniture in the entire house and I knew I was being vain, idiotically vain.

So I put my cup of tea down, which in itself was

something that happened about once every two million years, as you can imagine, and got up. She thought that was it then, they'd be eating off the carpet, and she lost it. My father's coming back from Spain next week, she was saying, won't you come back then, we'll have paid some money by then, please. I mean, I heard that every single day, that was nothing, but nobody had tried to take me to bed as well. Four or five kids in the house at the same time to boot, and she didn't seem a bad sort, not rotten.

'Forget it,' I said when I got back to the van. 'They settled it at the office this morning.' My colleague hadn't been doing this as long as I had so he just grunted something and we drove off, with it right there for the taking, the furniture and the woman. Maybe, I thought, I could go back later and strike something up legitimately, seeing I was a nice guy now.

I went back that evening, as it happened. Come four or five o'clock our manager went through the call sheets, which he usually did once or twice a week, and he came up to me and asked what had happened to 42 Havelock Drive.

'Nobody was in.'

'Well, go back now. There'll be somebody there now. Come on, you know better than that, we really need to tighten up on these cases. You know that they're coming down on us about our targets.'

Just about everybody else had gone home, and this man was adamant I go back to Havelock Drive and collect four items of heavy furniture on my tod. It went right up to the line, in fact, and I wasn't going to lose another job; I was already too old for that. Of course, there was a bloke there now, some husband or boyfriend, and he was up and at it as soon as he saw the van. In these instances it's best to skip the banter and drop them straight away, if you can, and I was able to do that then. So down he went and I nearly broke my back trying to get it all in the van before he got up again. I could hear her crying from the upstairs window throughout the whole thing. I'd spent long enough getting her to stop the first time, so God knows how long it took after that.

I went back to the lock-up, deserted by then, and left it all for some other bastard to unload. I'd had enough of it. It didn't take a lot to see that we were working on new rules after that, and things only got worse. Believe me, they did. There wasn't much I could do about it except starve, until Bruce.

As it happens it was Bruce who told me about Executive Lines. It sounds like a massage parlour, but it's a bit more exotic than that. I wasn't too sure where it was, so I spent half the morning criss-crossing the streets, and sure enough I drove past 42 Havelock Drive. Quickly. I saw plenty of old haunts that day.

When I found the shop I knew why it had taken me so long: it was on the first floor of a wareless warehouse, and its only fixed link with the public domain was a single-line entry in the business directory and a brass plate on its faded blue door the size of a pack of playing cards. It's one of those places that are only there if you already know them: there are a lot of those in St Pauls.

Bruce had only been there once himself, to get a price for a radioactive contraband detector that could pump gamma rays through the cavity in a car door. Drugs, weapons, explosives, anything that was meant to be hidden. The list price had more zeroes on it than was realistic, and after half an hour's haggling he was only able to shift it from being starkly unattainable to something merely laughably over-budget. The police can't afford to go shopping in Executive Lines, he'd moaned, only the sodding bastards we're trying to catch. Well, I felt like saying, here I am.

I remember him telling me about some portly Etonian old boy, but the person sitting behind the desk now was a big square-shouldered Arab with a moustache almost as large as his face, and a past equally as mysterious as his predecessor's. When I arrived at the top of his stairs, trying to catch my breath, he folded up the foreign newspaper he was reading and waited for me to speak. For a brief moment I considered what angle I was going to take, but then I chucked it in. I was out of my depth and there was no point in laying on a front. These people have always seen it all before.

'I need some sort of covert audio and visual recording system,' I said.

'What on earth for?' he asked, pretending to be curious. He was taking the piss, but still, it was nice to see someone in retail enjoying their job, and he could have used me for stand-up material for all the clout I carried. He could have thrown custard pies at me if he'd wanted to; there was nowhere else for me to go.

'For business,' I said. I could at least try to hold my ground.

'Indoors or outdoors?' he asked, suddenly professional, for which I was grateful.

'Indoors.'

'Mm-hm.' He nodded, and threw me a pack of cigarettes I actually managed to catch. I took one and passed them back; he took one too and we lit up. Then he put the cigarettes down on the window sill.

'Look at this,' he said, reaching for a box file on the shelf behind him. He opened it and took a sheaf of papers from the top. Underneath there was a five-inch LCD television and a nine-millimetre video-cassette recorder. He turned them on, and there on the tiny screen I could see my car in the street outside, below the window sill.

'Pinhole lens,' he said.

He went over to pick up the cigarettes and pointed the pack at my face: on the screen in the box file I saw my haggard features appear, looking baffled.

'See, it focuses. You like?'

I was speechless. He waved his hand over the front of the pack and I saw a giant palm hovering on the screen.

'In Marlboro, in the letter b,' he said, and after close examination I found a mark so small I knew that pinhole was no exaggeration.

'How does that work, then?' I said, feeling like an old Gwynedd granddad enquiring about a toaster.

'Video-link microwave transmitter in the bottom of the box file. Good for about nine thousand yards. You can pick it up in the basement, outside the building, in the building next door, whatever. Frequency is 1,250 megahertz, give or take a few. You have access to a high-gain aerial, you could be thirty kilometres away.'

Most of that went over my head like a passing plane.

'Will it pick up sound?' I asked.

'No. We need to get you something else for the audio, but it's not a problem.'

'And if the lights are out?'

'High-resolution camera. Low light levels are OK. Pitch black, no; nothing would work unless you go for infrared and that's not so easy to hide. Picture quality not so good either.'

'All right,' I said, remembering how Delia liked to keep the lights on, then forgetting again as quickly as possible. 'Does it have to be a pack of fags?'

'Cigarettes no good? OK. We have them in

clocks, smoke alarms, whatever. You tell us what you want and we make it for you.'

There wasn't enough time for that. The smoke alarm sounded good. If you put it on the ceiling you'd get better photography than in your average porn film.

'Let's have a look at a smoke alarm,' I said. The Arab passed me what to all intents and purposes looked like your standard smoke detector. Then he flicked a couple of inconspicuous switches and my face appeared again, as haggard as before, on the LCD screen.

'Works properly as a smoke detector too.'

'All right. And the sound?'

'That's nothing at all. Here.' He took a Parker ballpoint out of the drawer of his desk and scribbled on the newspaper with it before passing it to me. 'The bug's in the end of the cap.'

I couldn't see it but I had no difficulty believing him.

'How much?' I asked.

'For the smoke alarm camera, the audio bug, and two separate receivers, video and sound. Hm.'

He made me wait for a few seconds.

'Fifteen thousand.'

'That's too much,' I said. Perhaps I wasn't that dodgy after all, if I couldn't afford it either.

'Don't criticize our prices.' He smiled. 'They are perfect. Everyone who really needs one can always afford it. Always.'

'You don't have anything cheaper?'

'Well,' he said, and sat back down at his desk. 'What can we save on? I wonder. You tell me.'

'I don't need anything fancy for the audio. Just a normal tape recorder would do.' I could hide that under the bed. 'I don't need one of those box-file receivers either. In fact, if we can separate the video camera and the video transmitter, the only non-standard piece of kit I'm after is the camera.'

'Eight grand. Special offer'.

'You don't rent this stuff?'

'No. I will take seven. That's it.'

'I can give you four right now.' My knees went weak when I realized what I was saying.

'Hey! You see any signs around here saying zero per cent finance? We don't do credit.'

'Listen, I think I can pay the rest within days, no sweat. I need them today; the job's this weekend. I'm not lying to you here. If you can't meet me halfway we both lose. You lose your sale, I lose my client.'

'You think so?'

I nodded.

'OK, then. I have done something like this once or twice before. It is as generous as I can be. You show me some ID, some proof of home and work address. I take your four thousand pounds. You get your equipment. I give you an invoice, payable on receipt, dated six weeks ago. You sign and date it, also six weeks ago. I don't get the remaining three thousand by next week I lodge

173

court proceedings first thing Monday after. How's that?'

It was pretty raw, as offers go.

'Let me talk to my client,' I said.

'Yes. You talk to your client. My name is Zach. Have a think about it, eh?'

Zach unfolded his newspaper and in minutes I was inside a phone box. At this stage of the game it was important not to give yourself time to think.

'Hello again,' I said. 'Llywelyn here.'

'To what do I owe the honour, Lou-Ellen?'

'Look, I think I've mentioned this already. It is highly unusual in this business to work without a down payment of any kind. I . . .'

'What about the money I gave you in your office?'

What had that been, a hundred quid? I couldn't remember. It had lasted about twenty-four hours.

'That was only a retainer. On a case of this nature most people would want a third up front at least. I . . .'

'I've already discussed this with you. We both agreed that . . .'

'In light, listen to me, in light of the very specific demands you've made of me, the video footage and all that, I'm not going to be able to carry this out unless I see some more money.'

'You seemed fine with the arrangement before.'

'The costing's had to be revised since this video footage has come into play. This equipment costs the earth. If you're happy with sound recording and photos it's not necessary, but you're the one that said you wanted video. You do want video footage, don't you?'

'You said it wasn't going to be a problem.'

'It isn't. I'm just going to have to ask you for something more substantial, if only to ensure you're serious. Three thousand would do it. That's only twenty per cent of the total fee.'

'And without this you can't get the necessary equipment?'

'Well, I wouldn't be prepared to. That's all I'm saying.'

'But you know how to use it, this equipment?'

'Oh yes.' How complicated could it be?

'All right,' she said, bowing at last to the reality of the situation. 'When do you want the money?'

'Yesterday.'

'OK,' she said. 'I can give it to you tomorrow morning as long as you show me the equipment. And a receipt.'

'That'll do. Nine thirty a.m. at the Hilton. Don't be late,' I told her, and hung up. I wondered whether she'd be able to identify this sort of thing when she saw it. Probably not. I drove around St Pauls until I found a branch of my bank and they gave me my remaining four thousand. In small clear plastic bags, out on the counter, in front of everybody. Banks.

Zach didn't seem surprised to see me puffing at the top of stairs again, or so soon. I, on the other hand, felt like a Vegas novice staking the mortgage on red twenty-two at his first sitting, without really knowing why.

'You're on,' I told him.

'Have you got the paperwork?'

My pockets were always full of paper; there would be something in there. I rummaged. A bank statement: no use giving him that. Rather keep that balance to myself. A complete inventory of the more suitable documentation produced the electricity bill for the office, a local supermarket mailshot from the flat and the forms from the car rental company. I handed them all over and threw in a business card for good measure.

Zach squeakily shifted his weight around on his chair and stroked his moustache.

'Hm,' he said, thoughtfully. I took the clear, cash-filled plastic bags out of my jacket and laid them quietly down on his desk. On the shelves around us I could see things like telephone scramblers and thermovision cameras. In a glass cabinet to my left there were miniature laser sights for hand-guns. There was no way any of this lot was going to have any social benefit whatsoever, but I bet there weren't too many restless nights among the manufacturers and salesmen behind it all. Getting your hands dirty means precisely that, and it was not their lot in life to ever use the things, to watch and record and review the grainy footage of a flabby back heaving between two paid-to-part legs. They had no reason at all to do something like that, something I'm sure was no less innocuous than any of the other uses people put their products too.

Time passed. Zach was not a man to be hurried and I suspect he was enjoying himself. I sat and stared at the money, my money, and wanted to be sick. It got me right in the guts and spread all the way down to my feet: I was doubling up. I had been upping the stakes on this job since it started, first Selby and Co. and now this. I was doubling up and it had never worked before.

'Hm. Fine,' said Zach at last. It's not easy to let that kind of money go when it's inches away from your face, scant seconds distant from the grubby lining of your pockets.

'Video camera in the smoke alarm. Receivers and transmitters unhidden, just in their casings. Standard mike. Seven grand, four grand down. Special offer. You're our millionth customer.' Zach smiled at his own little joke. I wasn't smiling at all. This was a career investment. There were a lot more entrapments ahead of me now, now that I was seven grand down. I knew then that I was planning to do this all year round, year in, year out. Funny how you can surprise yourself like that.

It took him a few minutes to print the invoice and get the stuff together and then I signed away the next three grand with my heart in my throat.

'The batteries are charged for the next ninety hours or so. The receivers will run off a car adaptor, and remember: you need anything else, you talk to Zach.'

I picked up the equipment, which was in a cardboard box marked 'Bananas – Fragile', and carried it down to the car, leaving Zach to his Persian crossword.

'Fuck,' I said quietly to myself once the driver's door was shut, once I had a bit of privacy. I was committed. I was as in as in can be.

CHAPTER 4

Even at a moderate speed the car seemed to bounce and lurch along the neglected tarmac of St Pauls like a living thing, pouncing reflexively on each and every pothole with a sense of unerring accuracy. I could only hold my breath while several thousand pounds' worth of precious equipment slid precariously around in the boot, and let the Rover weave its own way through the inner city. I didn't really want to leave. I wanted to stay there until the ambulance ferried me out. I had done it before, in the inevitable binges that followed Bruce and McKellan. There are bars here that never close, bars you'd never know existed until they called for you: knock three times on the door, that sort of deal. I'm sure every city has them, and I wouldn't say I knew them well, but I knew them well enough.

They were full of small-scale drug dealers and pimps and other minor criminals, and they weren't shy about it either, although I never got talking properly to any of them. They liked to present a closed front, but the sheer shaken state of me was normally enough to establish my credentials, that and a sly twenty-quid note on the way in. It is a different matter entirely to drink in a pub that never has to close, and those places had almost been the death of me. As the Rover bounded down the back streets of St Pauls I kept expecting to see a familiar alleyway or basement door, but no bells rang. Now the bars were invisible, and I could have been in the arse-end of any rough city in the country. My hard-won insider's knowledge was out of date and the watering holes had moved on, either that or I had never been sober enough to remember where exactly they were. They would appear again, though, whenever the time came, you could be sure of that. I tried not to think about it.

Somehow or other the electronics and I managed to make Cotham, the neighbouring studentland, in one piece by the time the pubs were opening. It was a small mercy but it still counted. I was on Old Whiteladies Road before I laid the Rover to rest in an empty roadside parking bay, and finally feeling too overstretched to risk it, left a pound in the meter. It was a telling sign but nobody was looking.

The nearest open door belonged to a bar called Havana, a colourful Cuban theme pub whose bright yellows and greens turned to subtler hues of vomit and bile once you'd breached its garish exterior. There was a bored young bloke pretending to do something with a mop when I walked in, the first customer of the day. It wasn't my usual dive but some days you don't feel like discriminating. In the end they are all the same, or similar enough.

'What do you want?' he offered, a friendly little opener that laid down the bartender/beer drinker dynamic. He served me eventually but I was told I'd have to leave if the bar manager arrived.

'We don't cater for your type,' he said, leaving me to draw my own conclusions, and slid me a bottle of fancy foreign lager I'd never heard of that cost me nearly three pounds. I waited until I'd got my change back before I told him how much I liked his uniform; his black dungarees and stripy shirt bedecked with wanky badges. He decided not to follow it up. Maybe I'd levelled us: he didn't say a word to me till I left, but I spent a few frightening seconds looking at myself in the floor-to-ceiling mirror by the dance floor and after that I knew what he'd meant.

I gave up trying to use the car keys to extract the lime from the bottle after the first thirty seconds. I could put up with a side salad if it was the first drink of the day and it went down all right, and stayed there, even if it did taste of Opal Fruits. It was all that I wanted. I polished it off in the time it takes to wind a watch, and then I was free to stare vacantly into space until I'd worked out how productive I could be with my life today.

I had to get into my flat. I couldn't go much longer without the slight sanctuary my gaff afforded without suffering some kind of breakdown, and despite my habit of leaving the more domestic chores until as late as possible I felt I had pushed this one close enough. Work had been pressing, but if I didn't get back to the flat soon I'd probably never get there at all, so I walked up the road until I found a pub where I wouldn't raise any eyebrows, an old Charringtons place not two minutes away, asked for the telephone directory, and picked the first name off the list. You don't have to be choosy, locksmiths aren't like plumbers or builders: either you can get in after they've gone or you can't. They asked me for directions, and deciding it would be best to let them follow me down I just told them to meet me at the pub, which the landlord reliably informed me was called the Old Halfpenny.

'We won't be able to send anyone over for about two or three hours,' the voice had said, but I had nothing better to do. I could rig the room in the Hilton up tomorrow.

The pub had some comfy-looking armchairs and a fake log fire, but it wasn't my style to get too settled. When you drink as much as I do you're allowed to take your communion right at the altar, and leaning on the bar or perching on a stool conveys the additional advantage of allowing you to kid yourself that you're only on a fleeting visit.

The landlord played it distant and disdainful until he saw the five hundred malingering in my wallet, and then he condescended to pass the time of day. By the time he broke my second note the sad bastard had to confide in me that he too was something of a successful businessman, and how much he'd picked the pub up. Bank managers take note: it's always a bad sign to hear landlords go on like this, especially in empty pubs. I have met enough open-faced liars running enough last-legged dives to know better than to keep looking over my shoulder for custom that never comes, and this was one such curacy.

That aside, he was smooth enough to work the magic that turned empty pint glasses into brimming pints, and I was happy enough to watch my money disappear as the blood grew warmer under his bullshit and his beer. Up to a point. The cavalry came just as he made his third offer to take me on a tour of his spotless, stainless-steel kitchen. There have been few occasions when I have been so pleased to see a man with a toolbox. Authoritatively, I peeled myself off the bar stool and told him to follow me across the river. The guy squirmed visibly, probably a family man, and I knew what was coming next:

'Are you sure you're all right to drive?'

'Yes,' I said, squaring up to him, 'I'm fine.'

'All right.' He nodded, disarmingly, whatever principles he thought he had dissolving. Well, I thought, as I sauntered out, I only hire a car two or three times a year, that alone has to significantly reduce the statistical possibility of me causing an accident. And maybe it's more popular than you might think, that kind of optimist's mathematics, because the guy hugged my tail-lights like he was on a bloody tow-rope all the way down to Totterdown.

I found some unused kerb space in the road next door to the flat so I put the car in it and waited for the locksmith in his little Nissan van to do the same. By the time he'd reversed himself in I had freed myself of the seat belt and was there for him on the pavement, a drunk man in control.

'Follow me. It's the street around the corner but you'd never have been able to park there. I was down the pub late one night and I lost my keys. There. Over there,' I said, pointing. He was a young and sober man; he could go on ahead and make a start. Or so I thought. When I caught up he was doing nothing more than rolling a needle-thin cigarette and leaning against the low wall where I usually leant myself.

'I thought you said this was a lock job,' he said, and nodded in the direction of my door.

'Yeah, it is,' I said, and held his gaze for a moment before I looked at the door myself. It didn't appear to be there any more. On closer inspection I found it was there all right, but it was laid out on the floor of the hallway, its window shattered and its frame splintered.

'It was,' the locksmith corrected me, fishing around his overalls for a lighter. I let my lower jaw hang loose while I spent another few seconds examining the entrance to my flat. Had I done this? Had I, in the throes of a homeless binge, kicked in the door of my flat out of spite and left it behind me to sleep in the car or the office or a hotel?

'Hang on a tick,' I said, and was all I could say. It was beginning to dawn on me that I must have looked like a bit of an idiot, and I left him sucking on his tiny, impoverished roll-up while I investigated. It was the sort of thing I had done in the past, kick in my own door. I had kicked in all sorts of doors in my time, but a bit of head-scratching and ineffectual shuffling before an apathetic locksmith and I was no closer to an answer.

'Well, I suppose I'm going to need a new door,' I concluded.

'Yeah,' agreed the man, apathetically, between token puffs. 'Well, I can't do that for you. That's a carpenter's job.'

'Is it?' I said, sinking fast.

'Yeah, and you're not going to get one on an emergency callout service. I can board it up for you in the meantime, if you like, but you're not going to be able to get in or out.'

185

'Really?' I said. The locksmith took it rhetorically and smoked on, but it was a serious question. I took this to mean that unfortunately it was all real, and that I had better do something, anything, for form's sake. 'Just give me a second to get some stuff out.'

I rooted through the mess upstairs for a few clean clothes but the wardrobe was empty and all I had to choose from was the greasy, trampled overspill around my drowning laundry basket. It took a while before I cottoned on that the mess wasn't all mine. I may live like a pig but I don't engage in wanton acts of destruction towards my own personal property.

The pithy contents of the kitchen cupboards were scattered on the dirty lino; half a dozen soup tins for an ailing stomach and a rusting Fray Bentos. The drawers of my coffee table lay overturned on the lounge carpet, although there had been little in them. The Embassy vouchers I'd forgotten I ever collected danced worthlessly in the draught, barely enough for an electric torch. The screen of my portable television was smashed, its entrails scattered about the room. No, I hadn't done this. Someone who knew where I lived had paid me a visit. It could have been a burglar who got pissed off I had nothing worth stealing, but I doubt it.

'It wasn't me,' I said, with some satisfaction, as he stubbed out his fag against the wall of my house.

'No?' he said, indifferently.

'No. Someone's had a go at my flat.'

'Want me to board it up, then?'

'Yeah. I suppose so.'

While he went back to his van I changed into the cleanest shirt and suit I had left. It wasn't much of an improvement, but it was positive action nonetheless. Then I went and sat on the low wall of my small concrete garden and smoked the last of my cigarettes while I listened to the man hammer about forty nails into my door frame.

'No one's going to get that off in a hurry,' he said, between nails, fixing up the fresh plywood that now blocked my doorway.

'No,' I agreed, wondering how happy the carpenter would be when he'd have to take them all out again. It wasn't much of a lift, though, not when the nature of events began to kick in. Somebody was after me for something, and I had no idea who it was or what they wanted.

'All in, mate, that'll be seventy quid.'

I would find out sooner or later, that much was sure. Unless I was dealing with a genuine sociopath. I handed over the money for his inflated fee without argument. My mind was on other things.

'Cheers, mate,' he said, folding up the notes, and tootled off. I heard his van starting in the neighbouring street. Then I was alone, again. The streets were silent, almost; you could just hear the faint sound of children playing in the primary school near Wells Road. At the end of the street the hill turned to escarpment and the city spread itself out before it. When I moved here I thought the view was amazing, but everything turns to wallpaper in time.

Today I watched it all on the broken-down bench that only the dogs ever used, and that in passing, the way they used everything. The traffic oozed down the same roads, the long trains slid smoothly in and out of Temple Meads, following the tracks that arced out into the countryside and beyond. People went about their business as normal. Salesmen knocked on doors, schoolkids smoked sly cigarettes, housewives heaved shopping about, tramps begged, labourers stood in small groups and did nothing. Where could you even start? The Bush, the Oxford, the Newfoundland and the Shakespeare were all within fifty yards of each other, and not more than five minutes from the scene of the crime. It was excuse enough, and none was ever needed.

My wallet was bulging and there was time enough left to think and drink it through, not, of course, that I did much thinking. I stopped off in all of them, fixing a doner kebab nosebag to my face for the walk over Windmill Hill into Bedminster. I managed to get half of it down me before the dark sky made good its promise and let loose the flood it had been talking of for days.

It fell hard and fast, and the kebab was dropped upturned on the fractured pathway at the top of Victoria Park while I stayed close to the safety of the big, dying oaks as I made my descent, taking what little protection they offered. There was a pub, I recalled, named the Cart Horse, down near the north-west corner, and I went for it like a Doberman who'd sniffed sirloin in the shopping bag.

I'll just wait for the rain to break, I thought, as I ordered, and ordered. The barmaid came out with a towel for me and the pints turned into chasers for double whiskies. The black sky bled, and the pools of filth at the storm drains grew till they swallowed whole streets. Cars sent waves of grey, street-sodden rainwater up against the pub windows, and I watched it dribble down the criss-crossed lines of fake lead-effect tracery like it was diesel.

I drank and waited and still the rain didn't break. The sound of its falling was too loud for the old men to talk over, so the whole pub shut up and stared into their drinks while the storm unloaded and the barmaid, surely not old enough to be anything other than a truant schoolgirl, kept them coming. I lit the wrong end of a cigarette and realized I was pissed again, with the comfort of evening not yet come. I couldn't even pretend I was passing the time any more. I had another Scotch and left, if only for another pub, hoping a change of scenery might drag me out of it.

It was a good old walk but by that stage the rain didn't bother me. I didn't even notice it. I waited for service at the bar in the Old Ship, under the fairy lights, and saw a puddle form at my feet, my clothes hanging from me like wet bandages. My glasses fogged. The pub was rough enough for it not to matter. I asked for a double Bells and a pint of Flowers with words that slurred into each other but they knew what I meant.

'Nice weather for ducks,' someone said.

'Who gives a fuck about ducks?' said someone else. It was a pub where people talked. I began to rise a little out of whatever it was I was in. The fire was going out, slowly, under the drink. Sometimes you excite it, sometimes you extinguish it, but for now, at least, it was going my way. I took a seat next to some fellow miscreants and we talked rubbish for a while. After an hour or two of this I would be ready for the White Hart, and the White Hart stood a good chance of being ready for me.

I bought my brother losers a drink and suddenly, for once, I was the man of the hour. I knew better than to put a round on the house, but yeah, I did spread it around a little. Our little group grew, and the talk flowed, the talk of men who had nothing to talk about, little or nothing they wanted to dwell on, just an empty, laborious navigation of life's rapids, avoiding the rocks. It was inevitable we should hit something eventually, given that our sole and ever present impetus was the scramble from silence, waiting always in the lulls and pauses with its own questions and answers. Before we knew it we were talking of work.

I was getting slack, I suppose, my alibis and evasions too loose for a man of my background. You cannot always sail smoothly over everything, not when recognition can glimmer dimly at you from any corner, when your face has a vendetta attached for many people. I still have no idea who he was; maybe that's why I didn't spot him sooner.

'Still thieving from poor bastards like me?' he said, and hostility began to light in those around him like a slow-burning fuse. I felt the onrush of the past whistling at my ears, as if the air pressure over the table had dropped. At times I think the past is the closest thing to destiny we have in this life, or stronger, at any rate, like somebody got it badly arse over tit back in the days of beards and togas. People cheat fate all the time, it seems, but nobody can outrun the past. The best you can hope for is a swift sidestep, leaving half a pint behind you, and that only buys you some time.

'I think you've got the wrong guy,' I said, jovially, but dripping with insincerity. 'Don't know what you're talking about. Now if you'll excuse me, I've got to take a slash.'

Outside, dusk was well under way, and the rain

was showing signs of letting up. I walked head-long through the puddles glowing pink in the nascent street light and wondered whether I was worth leaving a drink over, half expecting the sound of hurried footsteps behind me. This had happened before, but a long time before. How could you recognize somebody after all this time? I was no longer in prime shape to rebuff or rebuke the victims of my old crimes with anything other than a hasty exit; the strength and speed were gone, and the spirit sadly indifferent. If it had happened tonight it would probably happen again, and that meant it would catch up with me even-tually. I didn't know what I thought about it exactly, but it bothered me, and when I walked into the White Hart the fire was up again. It wasn't as if I'd made a killing, I was only after the basics, enough to keep me in beer and nothing more. Why couldn't they let it go? The door slammed against the side wall and I left it to swing shut behind me.

The barman pretended to ignore me at first, but I was part of the furniture in there and you couldn't turn a blind eye to that. Not when I was leaning far enough over the bar to drool in the slop trays, crazy drunk, unwashed, trembling with I don't know what, the anger or the drink or sheer physical deterioration, who knows. My pint was dumped on the woodwork with a meaningful thud.

'Someone broke into my fucking flat,' I slobbered.

'Someone has fucking had a go at my flat. Where I fucking live. My fucking flat.'

'Well, it wasn't me,' someone said, taking the piss.

''Snot funny,' I said petulantly, sounding like the classroom gimp and feeling like a victim.

There could have been more jokes at my expense but I guess I looked mad enough for them to keep it behind my back, either that or I just didn't hear.

'Have you paid Declan back?' asked the barman, unimpressed.

'No. Not yet,' I said, and retreated to the fruit machine before he could so much as tut. I fed in the change, and kept feeding it in, while the drums spun and the lights flashed. I was too preoccupied to become interested and too pissed to play, but it was the only place I could stand where I looked like I belonged. I stayed there all night, leaving the spot only for more booze. Until, that is, I made a connection.

I wedged myself into the bar again.

'Declan been looking for me, has he?'

'Yeah,' uttered the barman.

'Pissed off, is he?'

'I'd say so.'

A suspect was beginning to emerge.

'That fuck,' I said, and the barman really did try not to hear. 'That little fuck,' I repeated, just to make it harder for him.

It was Declan's style, all right, just kick down the door and help yourself. At least the bugger couldn't have got his hands on anything: I had nothing of worth. No guessing where my money goes. So he smashed the place up a bit, which must have been frustrating for him because I'd already done all I could to fuck the place up myself. All for a hundred lousy quid. Declan, you bastard.

I was smug and righteous and raging, but all the fruit machine could do was blink back. I stacked up another tower of coins and slid them in. Declan would be here sooner or later. I had no idea what I was going to do, but I was going to do something and I was feverish to do it.

Declan turned up, as I knew he would, but not before forty or fifty quid had gone into the machine. Of course, he saw me first. I could hardly see anything by then, so it was hardly surprising. What was surprising was that he was the one to go on the offensive. I was nudging the third bar into place for a five-pound jackpot when a firm hand landed on my shoulder and swung me squarely about. I say squarely, but in my condition I was barely able to stand on my feet, so he put me in a headlock.

'Where's my fucking money?' he hissed.

'What do you mean, where's your fucking money? You've got some fucking nerve, boyo. Now let go of me before you get yourself into trouble.'

His headlock grew a little tighter.

'Where's my fucking ton?' he spat, through clenched teeth.

'You shouldn't go breaking into people's flats,' I gasped. 'It's bad luck, know what I mean?'

Declan threw me back against the fruit machine. I wasn't steady enough to stand without it, so I stayed there.

'What the fuck are you talking about, you mad old fuckwit? Now give me my money or you'll get a kicking the likes of which you've never seen before.'

'Too late. I was going to give it you, but you tried to help yourself, didn't you?'

'What?'

'You won't see a penny now. I'm not going to hand over money to someone that's had a go at my own place.'

'What? I haven't touched anyone's flat.'

Then he landed a backhand to one of my temples. My head jarred back and hit the corner of some wooden wall fitting. I was too drunk to feel a thing.

'I don't care if it was you or one of your mates or whoever,' I said, 'you can kiss your money goodbye. Have you got any idea how much the repair work's going to cost?'

It was not an approach Declan had expected, but he didn't give a toss about any approach that wasn't a fistful of tenners in his face. I began to twig that he and I were on a two-way street. I'd put him in a position where he'd have lost face if he hadn't lent me the cash and now he'd lose face if he didn't get it back, immediately, and with simpering gratitude.

The theory was confirmed when I received a few more smacks to the face, which soon became a flurry of knuckles that kept my head bouncing off the fruit behind me like a speed-bag.

'Where's my money?' he barked, over and over, and I began to get seriously unsteady.

'Outside!' yelled the barman.

'I'm not going anywhere,' I said, to no one in particular.

'Outside!' he yelled again. The punches didn't stop. The violence was beginning now; before that Declan had just been trying to sober me up.

Then it was the barman's hands which were gripping my shoulders, and I found myself moving towards the door. It was me who was being thrown out. He let me wheeze against the door post for a while and then I got a foot in the centre of my back that sent me sprawling against the pavement. I landed chin first and heard a few teeth go. I was lucky not to bite my tongue off.

'I don't like you, you Taff sheep-shagging cunt,' he said. 'I've never liked you. You're worthless. And do you know what?' he went on, in the same vein, 'no one likes you. The only thing worse than bastard scum like you is bastard scum who think they're welcome. Fuck off back over the bridge, you Welsh prick. You're barred. I mean it this time. If I see you around here again it'll be Johnny who'll take you to pieces, and I'll join in. There'll be nothing left of you. Don't let me see your face again.'

It was the longest speech I'd heard him make. Then he went back in to pour more wordless pints and Declan took his place. I was still trying to get up when I got the kick in the ribs; after those he moved on to the face, and pretty soon after that I passed out, to what sounded like my own bones breaking.

When I came to I could hardly move. My body had seized into a knot of pain. I ran my hands over my pockets as slowly as I could and they were all empty. The car keys, the wallet, the envelope full of money: all gone. I could tell from the carry-on behind me that the pub was still open, and doing a roaring trade. It looked like I was buying a few rounds on the house tonight after all. I crawled a little farther down the road, as far away from the White Hart as I was able, and every inch sent a jolt through me. I dropped into a shop doorway and waited to pass out again, knowing that when I came to a second time it would be even worse.

It was true, but before it could happen these blokes were walking down the parade five or six abreast, and when they stopped I could see they were the crowd from the Ship.

'Someone's got you already, then,' said the one with the grudge, looking down at me prostrate on the pavement. All I could see, and it terrified me, was this pair of steel toecaps. 'Do you know what it's like to have someone storm into your house and take what he pleases? Like you're nothing?'

Yeah, I realized, I guess I did now, but it didn't matter and neither did anything else. He started with the boot, like I thought he would, and I'm not sure what he followed up with. I think it must have disappointed him, me slipping out so easily, but I know he didn't let it stop him. When my eyes opened I was trembling like a leaf. The pain and booze and cold had meshed together and I was pretty sure I wasn't going to make the morning.

I had no idea what time it was, but from street level (literally, with my head on the kerbstones) the city's glow was still bright enough for you to watch the clouds creep over the rooftops. Slowly and surely they came, but their shapes were ever changing and they followed a pattern that never repeated itself and was known to no one. There is always something waiting around the corner for all of us.

It had stopped raining but my clothes were still wet, and it wasn't just water. I could feel it sticking to my tentative fingertips, a small, vermilion pool gathering steadily on the slabs. I saw it collect underneath an uninterested sky to a respectable size before I passed out for a fourth time.

Next thing I remember the sky was gone and the street lights were burning. I was in exactly the same place. In all that time not one person had approached me, or probably so much as looked at me, not without pretending they were looking somewhere else. They knew better than to bother with my type down here. It was something I'd always appreciated after previous closing-time embarrassments, being able to stagger bedward in semi-dignified isolation. Tonight I was too hurt to stagger and my bed was on the other side of two inches of plywood. Until the shock subsided the only movement in me came from involuntary tremors.

Of course, I can't say what happened that night with pinpoint precision. I ducked in and out of consciousness a dozen times, and whenever my eyes opened I was out of my mind. What can I say with any surety? I was alone, incapably drunk, after the worst beating of my life. Nobody's fault but mine either, and running through it all the knowledge that now I had been ostracized by the ostracized. I wasn't too sure where people went after that.

I managed to move myself eventually, to cover a little distance, and I'm pretty sure that I fell into the first of several shouting fits at the corner of Consort Road, letting the steam out at whoever I thought might be listening.

I know I spent a good while on the low-slung pedestrian walkway they have there, gazing fix-atedly at the Avon like it would rise up and answer me. It was there that the swing from anger to despair took place, and by the time I rang for an ambulance I was probably sobbing in the phone box. I'd definitely turned on the waterworks when the nurse gave me my medical blanket in the casualty waiting room in Redcliffe Hospital, surrounded by my true peers. I wasn't the only fuck-up in there trying to sleep it all off that night.

There were a dozen of us, curled up like groggy foetuses on the tiles, trying to hide under the bright orange bolted-down chairs from whatever our problems were, every one of us aware that our lives were fucked now, and that they were going to get worse anyway, regardless. In all my years in Bristol, with all the things I'd done and been, I'd never seen this before. It was the end of the road, right in your face.

There was something else, too. It was like a vision. I wasn't sure it had happened, but if it had been a dream I don't think I would have remembered it. Some time in the early hours I opened my eyes to see Detective Inspector David Knight, Bruce's successor on the regional crime squad, towering wordlessly over me with DS Gilboursen in tow. Leering without emotion, like I was an animal under glass. Like they were watching the final reel of the film, the tale running full circle, and they were not surprised. They just looked on with an almost scientific intent, and when my eyes opened again they were gone.

It was seven or eight when I came close to something like waking up, with my clothes stained with blood and piss and vomit. The place reeked and my room-mates, whoever they had been, had left already. As soon as I figured out where I was I just wanted out as well. A pity, really, as I think it was my last chance to wake up next to another human being.

'The triage nurse will see you now if you like,' said a spotty girl behind a plastic screen.

'No, I've got to go,' I said through the perspex, and stumbled out into the grey drizzle of morning. The streets were still empty and the cold morning air was crisp on the gums. It felt like a mountain breeze after my night in the waiting room. I ran my tongue around my mouth. The teeth at the front, the incisors or whatever they're called, were still there. A little chipped, that's all. A canine had gone and the one behind that, but my mouth wasn't bleeding any more. It felt like at least one of my ribs was fractured, and I couldn't unclench my right hand, which hung limply at my side like a growth.

I saw myself shiver but didn't feel it. I was dazed. But my feet shuffled slowly off to some unknown destination, manacled to an invisible chain gang, and for my part I just tried to stay as close to the wall as I could. I crept across half the city like that before a bench appeared, but rest wouldn't come. I was too tense, too wired, too near the precipice, and my strangely propelled zombie body seemed adamant it should be somewhere else. I let it, it being under the impression it could take me somewhere better.

Out came the first of Saturday's happy shoppers. How I envied them all, how I burned with jealousy. They had marriages and mortgages and families and friends and jobs, and even if they hated it all, even if they felt like they were drowning in their own lives, they had more than I ever will. I wanted to smash their fucking windscreens in one by one. I nearly did it but there was nothing at hand I could throw.

My feet lumbered on. My broken hand clawed at nothing, my head throbbed like a giant artery, my sodden swollen guts churned like cement in a mixer, the last alveolus in my charred, barren lungs began to blink out, and still my feet dragged the whole sorry mess of me onward, one grating step at a time. My pockets were empty, my flat boarded up. The pasty-faced drivers in their freshly pressed clothes sat motionless in their cars while hot, stale air circulated around them. Bitterness, I thought, has finally caught up with me, pure and strong and simple, a hangover that took forty years to instil.

I crawled on, obliviously, spitefully. Then, at the top of the road, the Hilton squatted on its blank, mirror-glassed haunches. I'd forgotten all about that place, or I thought I had. I wasn't sure I wanted to remember, but what else was there? If only the warmth, the shelter, the bar and mini-bar and room tab, and the cast-iron certainty they'd throw me out as soon as look at me. Mrs Dixon was due at half nine, which wasn't too far away, but if I stood rooted at first it was only because I had nowhere else to go. And when I edged closer, it was because I could only remember the parts I wanted to, like a burnt moth, dreaming he's still circling a candle now extinguished.

The doorman shot me a warning glance so I backed off, to wait in the council car park at the end of the street, not thirty or forty yards away. If I waited any nearer they'd move me on, or worse, call the police. I stayed shivering in that car park for the best part of an hour before I shifted my watch to within a cautious twenty paces of the hotel entrance. The doorman stared at me with fury from under his top hat but that was all. When I waved frantically at Mrs Dixon in her white Mondeo he nearly came over and knocked me flat. It wouldn't have taken much effort. Thankfully, she came stalking out on her stilettos before he could even raise an arm.

'What the fuck have you done to yourself?' she demanded. She showed little surprise, if any.

'Good morning,' I managed.

'You even smell like shit. Have you pissed yourself?'

'It could easily have been someone else,' I ventured. Mrs Dixon looked over my shoulder like I wasn't there, disgust creasing her face.

'Have you got your equipment?' she said finally.

'Yeah.'

'Well, can I see it?'

Oh God.

'Not right now . . . I ran into a spot of bother last night and . . .'

'You drag me over here at half nine in the morning and expect me to hand over three grand to this, do you?' she cut in, sharply. There was venom in her voice but she wasn't making a scene. She just stood there in disbelief, her hands on her hips, awaiting a reply. All five foot nothing of her. Somewhere in the distance a set of tyres screamed to a halt and horns sounded. A mild morning shunt, that's all, no broken bones or rushing sirens. I coughed up something thick but I didn't want to start hacking in front of her so I swallowed it. It tasted of blood.

'Yeah,' I said, because I could think of nothing else to say. I was barely capable of any kind of thought at all, but after a night like I'd had you needed to take it out on somebody. And it was that pent-up momentum which carried me, that alone. 'I've taken a big risk on you, missus. I've bent over backwards. You won't find anyone else who'll take on a job like this without some kind of money up front, real money, I mean. So I've been working my arse off, pooling my resources, and due only to circumstances beyond my control, and purely that, I have to ask you for some kind of deposit. Which is perfectly normal. And now that I am fully committed to this, you won't show me any commitment at all?'

I paused for breath, aware I was practically

shouting now. Fuck it, I thought, and shouted properly.

'If you can't at least show me that, I'm going to fucking tell him. Try getting someone to lead him to bed after that. And he'll believe me, oh yeah, don't worry about that. In fact, come to think of it, how much do you want for me not to tell him? Huh?'

It was a mad, furious ramble, the venting of grievances that had really very little to do with her, but she didn't know that. So although I shook her up quite badly it was due to the fateful timing of my release rather than any special talent. She stared intently at me, saying nothing. The words had sprung from my mouth as soon as they'd surfaced in my head, but in the face of her silence I nervously double-checked and they still sounded like a viable bluff. I left the ball in her court.

'Well, you have a point, of course,' she said.

'Listen, Mrs Dixon,' I said, leaning close enough for her to smell me, to catch the spittle and gag on the evil tide of my breath. 'I know I have a point. The only real question here is how much money do you have?'

'Walk a little with me,' she said, and headed off in the direction of the car park where I'd loitered in the freezing cold for an hour, and there the two of us stood alone, openly getting the measure of each other, me open mouthed and confused while she smiled coyly. I don't think it took her very long.

'What?' I asked, sensing something lurking around another corner.

'That prostitute you slept with Thursday evening,' she began.

'How do you know about that?'

'I paid for it, you stupid idiot. Why on earth do you think she jumped into bed with you, an attractive young girl like that?'

'Because I paid her as well.'

She laughed then, a quiet laugh that came in sharp, harsh bursts, like someone firing crystal decanters at a distant wall.

'What a girl! When, anyway, she was in the police station about seven hours later, so she could report her rape . . .'

'Fuck off,' was all I could say.

'. . . they gave her a thorough examination. All her bruises and so on, which looked very realistic, to her credit. They've taken swabs, too. For DNA records, I believe. You're on file already. They just can't put a name to it, and that's a small step, wouldn't you agree?'

'For a rape conviction? It's a quantum leap,' I said. 'She's a common prostitute.'

'We both know she wasn't common. As for prostitute, well, that's slander.'

'What have you got on me, then, rape or slander? You can't have both.'

'Rape, I think. Don't you?'

A startling but not necessarily serious turn of events – I could take all this in my stride: this was just a greedy little hustle from a woman with an inflated opinion of her own abilities. Nobody had ever tried to use my own methods on me before, but this was nothing, provided she could be made to understand it was nothing. Even if she knew it already, that small coy smile had to go.

'No chance,' I said, trying to talk some sense into her. 'Where would you start?'

'Where would *she* start, you mean. Well, as I've said, she's already reported the crime. All she needs is a witness here or there maybe, or some corroboration of evidence, a tip-off or two. My friends on the police force will be only too happy to arrange all that.'

'You have friends on the police force?' I said. If she was right about all that she probably did have a chance, especially considering my popularity with the local bobbies, but I decided she wasn't. She couldn't be. 'You'll need more than friends.'

'Oh, I don't know,' she said. The smile was still there, and it was a lot less coy now. 'They're very good friends.'

'If you can find somebody on the force who'll stick his neck out over a rape frame as phoney as this, you're welcome to try. I have to admit there's a statistical possibility you'll succeed. It won't stop me from telling your husband, though, will it?'

'Who says it has to come to that? All I want is the job done. I'm a woman of my word: I want the job done, I want it done tonight, and, as I've mentioned, I can't pay you a penny more until that happens. This is something I've made clear from the start.'

'That's not what you said when we spoke yesterday morning, though, is it? And I'm expected to believe, after this little trick, that you'll just hand over my full fee? That girl can't have been cheap.'

'I wouldn't know. She was worth it, though, just to underwrite your services, shall we say. I don't think she was too dear, but then I drove her down quite a bit: it's easy when your libido isn't opening your wallet.'

'Whatever you paid her, I'll be needing more money if you want me to do the job, and that's final.'

'I'm sure you can find it from somewhere, a man of your resourcefulness.' Then came that laugh again. I was a man half crippled and covered in the dross of the street, stranded in a council car park with a housewife who believed she had a reasonable chance of putting me away, and who was half right. I didn't think it was quite as funny.

'Do you know what?' I said, and I needed to say this, I needed to say it very quickly before the consequences sank in, before my cheapness sold me out or my nerves faded. Before I had to hear her laugh again, because if I heard it again it would be for a long time after it had stopped. 'This isn't worth it. I never wanted to do this fucking job in the first place. I'm jacking it in.'

She didn't reply to that. She didn't beg, or plead,

or hand over a cheque, and so I had to walk all the way out of there with nothing but my pride. It wasn't nearly enough, and I had to tell myself I'd give her an apologetic call later in the day just so I could keep moving.

PART III

EXECUTION

CHAPTER 1

I spotted it from the pavement, walking back to the flat with no idea how I was actually going to get into it: a steel crowbar about four and a half feet long down by the junction box. For shifting railway sleepers, or something. The fencing round there hadn't been touched in years, and even a man of my bulk could squeeze effortlessly through the wires, hanging slack on posts loosened by the rain-soaked soil. Then I put one foot on to the soggy mud of the embankment on the other side and fell instantly, sliding down to the tracks like a broken toboggan. When I reached the thing, the object, it was so heavy I nearly toppled over backwards. Not the most appropriate tool, granted, but beggars can't be choosers.

Only when I tried to bring it back to street level did the scene really descend into bleak tragi-comedy. I don't know how long I spent down there, but the outside world soon became a distant memory, a previous life. Numerous times I reflected fondly on it, the way people look back on their childhood. Whenever I found myself lying on my side, say, wiping the slime from my face with one unbroken hand while my booty rolled slowly but irretrievably away. Then, like Sisyphus at the summit, it was downhill to get the boulder back. I might as well have been climbing the Matterhorn on roller skates, and I was lucky, if that's the right word, that there weren't any trains.

I made my return to the roadside after more attempts than is believable, forcing my way through the rusty chain-link, more difficult too this way round, from a lower position, and the only thing stopping me from kissing the tarmac when I got there was the terrible and also embarrassing knowledge that I still had to get it up to Totterdown, but I managed it, even if my hands were blistered like bubble-wrap by the time I dragged it into my street.

The boarding came off as if it had been stuck down with sticky tape, and most of the door frame too. The whole thing was buggered now, but that was the least of my problems. I stepped into the hallway, which now looked like someone had led a panzer division down it, and went upstairs. I found half a pack of forgotten Camels in my coat and they were stale as sawdust but it was all I could do to stop myself eating them for breakfast. Then I coughed for the next twenty minutes.

By rights I should have gone to bed then, and slept like a baby. Got a few hours in before the end of the afternoon. Except I was too highly strung to want my eyes closed for long, and too tired. I'd overstretched myself into that hollow-headed unblinking state of automated motion that never ends until you collapse outright. If I was going to sleep properly it would be after this business was all over, however it ended. I wondered nervously how long I should leave it before ringing Mrs Dixon. I didn't want to leave it too long or she might write me off, and then what? I'd heard about what happened to sex offenders in the clink. It wasn't about rehabilitation, or repentance, or punishment: they just destroyed you. So, knowing rest was impossible, I decided to go through the old routine once more. For old time's sake.

Undressing was a reptilian affair, like shedding an old epidermis. I don't know whether it's as painful for snakes. I put the shower on full blast, nothing more threatening than a steady drip, and gave it ten minutes. I watched the events of the last few days gather at my feet as they swirled downward to the void. Piss, blood, vomit, food, sweat and mud all congealed briefly around my feet before vanishing for ever. It didn't really feel like it made much of a difference.

I went over to the cabinet, callously dripping on the lino like a wet dog, and took out the toothbrush as if I'd never seen one before. I gave the throbbing gums a few soft strokes but even that was too much, so I swilled and forgot about it. I tried to unclench my bad hand but it wouldn't budge. My bruises were as purple as plums. There were weeping cuts over both my eyes which had barely scabbed over. Teeth were missing. A rib didn't feel like it was in the right place. It hurt to breathe.

I shaved one-handed. The mirror lay in pieces on the floor so I don't know whether I did a good job, but the sink was clogged when I'd finished. And my scabs had started bleeding again. At least people would be too busy staring at my face to notice the state my shoes were in; I would have looked smarter if I'd taped bin liners around my feet, but I didn't bother. I scavenged around the back of the sofa and the pockets of a few old clothes and came up with a tenner or so in change. If I was lucky it would last, if I could stay out of the pub, which was already beckoning.

Then I grabbed my coat, glad of a bit of warmth at last, and that was it. Not much point in sticking around any more. I hobbled out, leaving the place wide open behind me. I had an inkling it might not really matter that much what happened to the gaff from now on, one of a few dark suspicions lingering behind the frontal lobes, but before I could get replacement keys for the car, or check the times with Delia or install the camera, there was Inspector Knight himself. Leaning back on the bonnet of an unmarked police Mondeo, looking a bit like an answer to questions I couldn't be bothered to ask, or was too cowardly to contemplate.

'Morning, old bean,' he said. Oh yeah: Dave Knight, like a few English people, had this thing about affecting phrases or expressions he thought were used by posher English people. He always added this kind of wry sneer to it too, which I could never decipher, and which may have been an attempt to pass the whole thing off as irony. I don't think it was irony, though, not from a sad bastard from St Pauls who started taking horse-riding lessons at the age of thirty-two. However, this is not important.

'Hello,' I said. I was already worried.

'Long time no see. Come on, we'll give you a lift. I think a chat is long overdue.' Not without some warmth, he opened the rear door for me. What can you do? Run away?

Julian Gilboursen was in the driving seat. He took a look at me in the mirror, my scabs and scars and bruises, and said:

'What are we going to do with you, eh?'

I smiled back at him, which I felt OK about, two old battlers still taking knocks and all that sort of cobblers. Gilbo pulled away from the kerb and Knight turned off the two-way radio, cutting us loose from station priority and protocol with a flick of the wrist. We rolled twenty-odd feet to the end of the street, turned into Arnos Vale cemetery, and came to a halt. The whole thing had taken about ten seconds.

'Out you get,' said Knight, getting out himself to open the door for me like an extremely polite taxi driver. I got out. The boot flipped open: Gilbo pulling a lever under the steering column. Knight gestured for me to climb in with the sweep of an open hand, as if announcing me to a formal dinner party. 'Hop in.'

I was scared. When I'm scared I usually have a good reason for being scared, even if I can't really put a finger on it, so I usually go with it. This time the reasons were pretty obvious; regrettably, it didn't look as if I could do much about them. I stood motionless by the boot lid, staring at the graves, frozen. Inside, I was doing all I could, using whatever concentration possible, to think about supermarkets, taking up cigars again, why the sky is blue, basic maths, anything. Like the open-mouthed moment in the surgery before the dentist's drill bites, with its watertight promise of imminent pain, to the power of ten. Knight got me between my shoulders and I toppled in like a rotten timber.

'Frightfully sorry, old boy,' I heard him say, through the thin steel. I waited for the rush of fear, the cold sweats and racing pulse, but it didn't come. My resting heart rate must be nearly a hundred as it is, and anyway, the boot wasn't so bad. I could have been quite happy, I think, if they'd just left me there. In my lightless cocoon. No stimuli, no stimulation: that's how it is with me, it dawned, I'm like an ostrich. Courage must be something like this, something similar, a variant of or distant relation to. It wasn't until the sky flooded in between the two head-and-shoulders silhouettes that the fear came back.

'Up and at 'em,' one said, and I sat up blinking.

Then they had me stumbling, an arm each, over uneven ground to some low bungalow ahead. No; a Portakabin on a raised platform. Lots of plants round the place. I clocked it was a garden centre before they got me inside, a hand on the back of my head to glide me through the door frame as they helped me up the concrete steps, the way you see them sliding suspects into the back of police cars on television. I've never seen anyone do that in real life, though, they just let them catch it on the crown, but this wasn't television, it was a bloody garden centre, and I wasn't a suspect, I was a friend, a friend among friends: this was one of the messages they were very keen to get across.

We went into an office off the tiny corridor and they showed me a scuffed chair of orange plastic. It was the only chair in the room. Knight sat casually on the edge of the only table, and Gilbo leant against the office door, having closed it, hands in pockets. All very casual.

'Well. You've got to be wondering what the fuck's going on,' said Knight, not especially insightfully. I had no intention of saying anything unless they asked a direct question. I didn't want to put my foot in it, at least not any more than I might have done already, that was one thing, and easily done when you are indeed at a loss to what the fuck's going on. That was one thing, but the over-arching reason for staying shtum was that I knew my petrified voice would rasp and crack like a broken reed, and it would be shameful, to show that this early on. But perhaps, I thought, there really was no need to be scared at all. Yeah, I thought, that diagnosis was worth trying for, and did what I could to hold course, but still said nothing at all.

'First off, what I want to say, and this is straight up, we're all mates here. So don't worry,' Knight went on. This was good, I thought, this was the stuff. 'If you fly off the handle you're no good to us at all. We need you. Don't lose your bottle. There's no call for that.'

Gilboursen took a packet of Regal out of his jacket, extracted one, lit it, and put them back. He didn't offer one to me. Or Dave. I launched instantly into a frantic calculation of the possible implications of such an act, which were limitless, and came no closer to knowing how harmful their intentions were. This would come out shortly, no doubt, but the process had kept me from falling to pieces for a time.

'Now, we haven't spoken for a long while. When they started looking into old Cookson, you know, our names were mentioned. I don't blame you for grassing, but you didn't do yourself any favours. We had to freeze you out after that. Couldn't be associated with somebody who was officially in cahoots with police corruption, could we?'

I nodded, very slightly, feeling a bit more reassured.

'That's all that was. Then this colleague of ours, and we all know her, has this job which needs doing and she goes and hires you. We didn't know this until very recently. We wouldn't have wanted her to hire you, frankly, no offence, but she did. As you're probably aware, she's a bit sharp. So she decided to come the cunt with you, didn't she? She set you up a treat, and you didn't like that too much, and you went off the handle because it was the only thing you could do. It's the only thing you can ever do.'

Knight paused and bit his upper lip, choosing his words carefully. Feeling sociable I nodded again, but nobody was looking.

'The thing is, what she's hired you to do is very important. Too important, really, for a fucking alkie like you, and too important, really, for a greedy little bitch like her to start getting clever over. So it could have been simple and now it might be very complicated, for all of us, depending largely on you.'

Outside I could see rows and rows of flowers – roses, chrysanthemums, lilies; I don't know the names of many flowers but there were a lot. Acres and acres of blues and reds and pinks and so on. Seemed pretty innocuous for this kind of scene, but dark rooms, empty nightclubs, abandoned warehouses: these things were never material. Only the fear is essential, and that was there.

'Have you got your equipment?' Knight asked.

'Yeah,' I said.

'Know how to use it?'

'Yeah,' was definitely the answer to give here. These were pretty easy so far, I thought. In fact, the whole thing turned out to be a walkover. I don't mean to sound arrogant or anything, but try and figure out what the best response to these was:

'You've still got time to install it?'

'This girl you've got, she's reliable?'

'Got the room booked?'

'Feeling up to it physically?'

'Foresee any complications, anything we might be able to help you with, say? Any problems at all?'

'Sure?'

'Cigarette, me good man?'

We puffed away then, the three of us, under a cloud of pacifying smoke. Full marks, no contention. In a seizure of optimism, wholly welcome considering all alternative outlooks, I concluded that this really had been nothing to worry about.

'We're sorry about your flat,' Knight said.

'That was you? You trashed the place.'

'No, we just forced an entry. If the place got messed up then it must have been kids. We did the office too but that was easy; we've had a spare key for that kicking around for years. We just had to check you out, you know, see if you had anything on us. Do you know what this is about?'

'No.'

'Didn't think so. That's as it should be. The thing you've got to keep in mind is that if you fuck this up in any way you're going to get yourself killed.

That's just how it is. Do you believe that? You know we've killed in the past.'

Again, this was a piece of piss:

'I know, yes.'

'Well then. I really hope nobody has to kill you, mate. So stay off the bottle for today and get this sorted. Don't do anything stupid. We thought we might have to do you here, that's why we brought you. There's a clay pigeon centre next door that would cover the noise, see, and this place is closed on weekends. Wholesale only, my dear chap.'

'Fucking dodgy places, garden centres,' said Gilbo, nodding sagely, and I felt the urge to laugh my head off, except if I let myself go I knew I would only burst into tears. There were lines I could have used here, I'm sure, being threatened with death in a wholesale garden centre. At the time, though, you tell it and take it as straight as you can. Anything else would be in poor taste, I think, when your head is on the block. My right eyelid began to blink uncontrollably, in idiot's Morse, and Knight looked out at the flowers while it ran itself down.

'Just what do you think you know about all this, if you had to come up with something?' he said, looking away politely.

'Nothing.' (Still on form here, obviously.)

'All right, take a guess. A wild guess. Do your best.'

'I really couldn't.'

Knight turned and glared at me.

'Stop being a prick,' he said.

'All right. It's blackmail. I don't think you'd care about fixing somebody's divorce settlement, so you must want him to do something for you.'

'Yeah, that's about it,' said Knight, after a lengthy exhalation. 'He knows one or two things he shouldn't, and something I think you already know about. Anyway, I think we're done here. When you've finished the job just go back to your flat with the tapes and we'll come round and sort the money out then. Come on, we'll give you a lift. Where'd you want dropping?'

'Let me think,' I said, my organizational skills somewhat impaired. 'Uh . . .'

The world outside was only just beginning to feed back into my reality, which had contracted to the size of a Portakabin office and had yet to expand.

'You can tell us on the way,' said somebody.

'What was it they had . . . that he had on you? That you think I already know?' I don't know why I thought I'd get away with that one. I thought they'd just clout me one, but it didn't happen.

'They found O'Connell.'

'The body,' Gilboursen clarified needlessly.

'We look after our own, right?' Knight said wearily, though not without a flash of pride, as we got back into the car. They let me sit on the back seat this time, seeing how they didn't have to kill me yet.

I got them to take me to Choice Autos on Old Market Street, once I was on an even keel, to get a new set of keys for the Rover. Knight said they'd wait around in case there were any problems and Gilbo parked up on the opposite side of the road with the engine idling. I didn't know what they planned to do if there were any difficulties, and I didn't really want to find out. Frankly I wasn't sure I really wanted to see them any more at all.

The Choice Autos forecourt was as empty as before, full of nothing but half a dozen unloved, unwanted motors. The same man was still there, in the same brown overalls. I suspect he had a pair for every day of the week: they were cleaner than any item of clothing I owned.

First I told him who I was and explained that I'd been mugged the night before. Then I asked for a new set of keys. I seemed to be speaking with some kind of lisp. Surely, once all this was over, I hoped, even a prison dentist would be able to do something with my teeth, my yellowing and freshly smashed gnashers.

'What happened?' he asked, and I knew I might have to do more talking than I'd thought. The important thing was to get the keys without having to hand over any money.

'Like I said, I was mugged.'

'Have you got a crime reference number? Have you reported it?'

'No, not yet. I don't see why it's any of your business if I choose to report it or not.'

'We need it for insurance purposes. I can't give a second set out without one.'

'Listen. I've been mugged. Fucking look at me. They took everything I had, right down to my digital watch, which didn't work. I was unconscious, I spent the night in casualty, and I need those keys. Hand them over, and if I don't have a crime number by the time I hand the car back you can put it on the bill.'

The man in the moustache shifted his weight slightly from foot to foot and said nothing.

'Come on, pal. It's been one thing after another for me these past few days.'

'All right,' he said, and while his eyes kept their blank, cool glaze, maybe his mouth showed a glimmer of compassion from underneath its well-trimmed tash. Or maybe he just wanted me out of the room. Either way, the guy was a saint. 'Sign here.'

I signed away; don't ask me what. Then I went out to the pavement and waved my new keys at the boys, so they'd know everything was on track, and they shot off with just a spot of wheel spin and not so much as a toodle-oo. Which was a pity, because I could have done with a lift up to Totterdown to get the car.

'I know that guy,' said Overalls, behind me. 'Bought a Honda Civic for cash last spring.'

'Wasn't black, was it?'

'Most of them are. What's he do?

'Oh, he's an entrepreneur,' I said. 'With a big blue pointy hat.'

I like to think it was the same car, and it made

a degree of sense. If that woman had let me follow the real Dixon around maybe I would have found out enough about him to get suspicious, maybe click to a few links between him and the old crew, and when she finally agreed to some surveillance she made sure it was only for me to end up trailing Knight or some other decoy who could easily give me the slip. But chiefly I like to think it was the same car because it means I didn't fuck up a simple tail job.

No one raised an eyebrow at the bus queue. I was reminded of something Maggie Thatcher said about public transport, about any man over twenty-six on a bus being a failure. As a rule I expect it had a lot of exceptions, but I wasn't one of them. I was off to hell in a handcart.

An elderly and frankly unstable spinster caused me some discomfort, not unintentionally, I'm sure. Normally I would have let her rest her pins on the pock-marked plastic but today it was all I could do to stop myself from pushing her away. I just sat with my hands deep in my empty pockets, stared straight ahead, and watched my breath cloud and disappear in the cold while she groaned shamelessly. The bus appeared after half an hour, which wasn't bad, and I bought a two-stop fare, hoping the driver wouldn't catch me travelling over my limit. It saved me enough to buy half a pint: no point in carrying airs and graces now.

In the street neighbouring my flat the car was where I'd left it, apparently unmolested, and pretty soon I was sliding my shiny new key into the driver's door with the heart of the city below me. The car reeked, and the foot wells, back seat and dashboard were covered in rubbish from my point-less stakeout days before. I barely noticed. It started first time, and it didn't begin to fade until I'd edged out into the steady stream of traffic that flooded down Wells Road. After a decent bout of heavy swearing I conceded that I hadn't filled her up once since I got her, and I glided into the Clarence Road Stop 'n' Shop on vapours, with hardly a tenner in the world. Fill her up and run for it, I told myself, but I wasn't up to such fast tricks in my state. Instead I spent a few deter-mined, concentrated moments with my hand on the pump, counting out two pounds' worth of unleaded. Two pounds. It felt almost as bad as doing a runner.

To top it off, the child behind the counter wouldn't accept my pair of pound coins.

'We only sell petrol for two fifty or over. That's the policy,' he said, and we both knew he wouldn't budge. He was too bored to let a little fun slip by.

'Why?'

'Because.'

'You don't want to turn a blind eye, just this once?'

'Not allowed, mate.'

'Don't "mate" me, you pimply bastard.'

'What did you call me?'

'A pimply bastard.'

So I was back in the yard with just the slightest pressure on the pump, willing shaking hands into a surgeon-like steadiness. A queue of thirtysomething suits grew at the entrance and I could feel the stares on my back. They had company Vectras, expense accounts, pensions, mortgages and ten years on me. Somewhere in the suburbs their three-piece suites had habitually imprinted on them the presence of their families, their wives and sons and daughters. They had things to do: they were people that did things. I was someone that things happened to, and I was trying their patience.

The pennies on the pump slowly ticked over and the pimply bastard stared on through the perspex across the way. Yesterday's tabloids fluttered around an empty bin. In the thick of my temple a bulging vein throbbed its own pulse, and overhead clouds rolled silently like poison gas across an empty battlefield. A bill had been written and payment was due. What had become of me? What was going to become of me? I didn't know. What I did know was real dread, for the first time in my life, on a petrol station forecourt in South Bristol aged forty-five. The disgust and apathy parted, and pure dread fell through in sheets. This was the real thing: I was going down, for crimes past, present and future, for transgressions real and imagined, for stuff no court in the land was wise or brave enough to convict me for, and I deserved it all. Somewhere inside me thirst flamed so brightly it looked like an alibi, but I knew that it wasn't.

My sentence was beginning, I realized, or had already begun. My life, if you could call it that, was over, and I had found out what the look in that photo had really meant. That photo of Mr Dixon, with those nervous eyes as unsteady as crutchless cripples, looking and watching and waiting for the fall. They had me now, and there was no reason to believe they would let me go unless it was to drop me like a stone.

I got my two fifty dead on the nail and left my change on the counter. The car sounded a lot happier when I turned the ignition and I headed off for nowhere again, unable to bring myself to put the camera in or check up on Delia just yet. There is still time, I told myself, there will be time, and I'd done a couple of circuits of the city before stopping at a corner shop to spend the rest of my money buying cigarettes through yet another plastic screen. The old guy who ran the place looked scared enough to justify it, although in my opinion if they want to get you they will. This perspex that you see all over the place, it's not to keep them out: it's to keep you in, to tell you that there's nowhere else that you can go.

Most of the cigarettes went in as many miles, and then when the need somehow seemed to spread from my bladder to my liver I had to leave the car on double yellows while I went into

230

McDonald's. It was so urgent it was dizzying, and after I'd unzipped I leant heavily against the tiled wall to try to take a few deep breaths while I was at it, but my chest was too sore to expand much. Then I looked down and I was pissing blood. I mean the urinal ran red. I recoiled, pissing on the tiles, and almost screamed (actually I just groaned, I don't think I was capable of anything more dramatic). At first I thought I might be hallucinating but I watched it lap and curl around the little yellow disinfectant blocks and it seemed fairly real. Even if I was hallucinating it meant there was still something badly misaligned internally, still something undeniably fucked up about me. In the mirror over the sinks I stared at my reflection properly for the first time in days, closely and unflinchingly, and my skin, where the violence hadn't touched it, was the colour of old marzipan. I walked out to the car without bothering to do up my fly and checked in the side mirror: under the neutral light of day it was no better.

I got back in the car again, which was the only place I could go, and started the engine. What I needed, I decided, and this will tell you a great deal about my general mental condition, was a bit of fresh air. A bit of fresh air and then on with the day. I took her over Clifton bridge and on to the downs, where I parked and left the heaters on. Up and down the lane people in Barbour jackets were lifting dogs better groomed than I was into and out of the boots of expensive estates.

When the coast was clear I turned the heaters off and eased myself out as painlessly as possible. The wind blew hard and cold over the bleak Clifton downs, and I grew numb in no time at all. My lungs and liver may have been in their last flashing throes, and my cuts and bruises still stung, but all else was the wind of the coming winter. I stumbled around a bit with my jacket collar up and my arms folded across my chest. Bristol lay complacently below the cliff-tops. The lazy Avon oozed through it and out the other side, through farmers' fields and market towns.

Inevitably, perhaps, I ended up on the bridge itself, the barrier between the city proper and the mess that sprawled away from it, the heartless retail parks and new housing estates, the slow seeping discharge all cities will pour forth on to the countryside that bore them. I was standing on the centre of the span, hands knuckle white around the safety rail. Through the Victorian latticework I could see the river a million miles below. If I was a different sort of person, I thought, this would be it for me, I'd be up and over and off. It was nice, in a strange way, to think about it, to toy with the idea. I knew I wouldn't. If I was going to top myself I could have done it years ago and saved a lot of bother all round. I was, I suppose, still stupid enough to hope. Too far gone to hope for something specific, for anything real, but just stubborn enough to harbour a little blunt faith inside me, like a kidney stone.

There was talk about putting steel netting over this walkway. The suicide statistics made the council a little edgy, cretins that they are. Let the poor bastards jump, if they've got the nerve, let them go. It was clean and it was quick. Far better for your broken body to turn up quietly in the rushes on the river bank than clog up the wheels of the Paddington express. Who wants to clean that up? Let them go, I say, if they've got it and if they've got what it takes. I didn't, so I was just killing myself as slowly as I could, and hoping I wouldn't notice.

Down below I could see some of the old docks, nothing more now than a few stakes stuck in the mud flats, the wood so soft you could tear out chunks with your bare hands. The steamers and coal ships and freighters made their last voyages years ago. Galleys full of slaves and then liners full of cloth-capped emigrants and then pleasure boats laden with underawed tourists and now nothing: it has all gone. It was low tide, and the river had receded to show its aching, litter-strewn sides to the world. I stood there and felt the world turn. I was trying to think of something, to formulate some kind of escape route from it all, but my mind had turned to lead.

There was nothing I could do but get back in the car and drive, and not stop. Things might work out, but they wouldn't, and even if I knew it I couldn't quite believe it yet. I couldn't reconcile myself to what lay ahead, and I would have driven all day, and I would have run out of petrol and money by mid-afternoon, but it didn't quite turn out like that. When I got back to the Rover my hands were shaking so much I had to work hard to get the key in the door and it was just as well, because before I could unlock the car I'd thrown up all over the bodywork, and there was nothing left in me to bring up. I was retching like a trooper, sliding across the front wing till my knees touched the ground, where I watched strands of luminous bile spew downward like spider's webs. My empty stomach spasmed, the withered abdominal muscles clenching weakly over a wide expanse of abused intestine.

I'd been through this a few times, years before, when I'd been drinking round the clock. I thought I was better now, but obviously there was still some way to go, and the reality struck like a fever, as sudden and unsettling as the spasms them-selves: I was in the clutches of regression. I knew, though, that the attack would pass in time, leaving me giddy and muddy kneed after about twenty heaving minutes, but after that I couldn't be sure. There would be more, maybe in the next hour, maybe all day long.

When my breathing was reasonably even I wiped myself down with my hands and lowered myself into the car, put the heaters on and wound the windows down. I still thought that maybe I could just drive around a bit, let the wind whip me into shape. But it was too late in the year and the wind up there in the Clifton heights was cold, and as sharp as broken bottles. It wouldn't have made much of a difference. I could see my own eyes in the driver's mirror and they needed more than a fresh breeze. I needed medical attention.

There was only one person I went to for that, and I'd always made a point of avoiding him, even when I could consider myself fairly respectable. He was a police surgeon and he worked out of the city morgue down by the student hospital in Redcliffe, or at least I hoped he did. Richard Jenkins was his name. I'd been to school with him, and he was the only person I still knew whose pedigree could be traced back to the old days, the only link I had with what had once been home and what had happened there. It was probably why I hated to be near him.

Bruce told me once about a murderer on death row in Alabama, or somewhere similar, a guy who was sixty-four before his last appeal fell through. He had a heart attack fourteen days before they could strap him into the chair. That man got the best medical attention the dollar could buy, doctors most free men couldn't afford. They made him alive again, they fixed him and nursed him and got him on his feet, although it took months. And then they sent him back to the state penitentiary, where he got his head shaved and his legs manacled and a leather bit stuck in his mouth and his arms and legs buckled down into the same old chair, so they could kill him the way God and America had ordained.

I felt a little like that, to tell you the truth, stumbling shyly over the stone steps of Redcliffe hospital past a dozen young doctors on a study break, all waiting for the day when they'd work eighty underpaid hours a week saving bums like me.

CHAPTER 2

Security didn't give me any bother because there was no security there in the first place. What every office block in the Western world took for granted hadn't been included in this budget, or if it had it was off having a cup of tea with some nurses. Not that I minded. It was the receptionist who had to apply the cold shoulder.

'Can I help you?' she asked, before the doors behind me had even swung shut, but she didn't want an answer. 'We don't handle in-patients in this hospital. If you want to get seen I'd suggest any of the other hospitals in Bristol.'

'I don't want treatment,' I said. 'Not right now, anyway. I'm making a personal call.'

'We don't take visitors here,' she said, with her arms folded firmly over her empty appointments book.

'No, I'm here to see a member of staff. I'd like to see Dr Richard Jenkins. Is he here today?'

'What did you want to see him about?'

'Like I said, it's a personal call.'

'He finishes at seven.'

'It can't wait.'

'Well, I'm sorry, this is a very busy hospital and Dr Jenkins is a very busy doctor.'

'Like I said, it's not a social call. It's very important and extremely urgent.'

I handed her one of my few remaining business cards. It was dog-eared at one corner and covered in pocket fluff, but like I said, they seemed to work every time. It was disappointing in a way.

The woman in white read it and looked up with shock now leaking through her stern, matronly severity. I'd given them something to gossip about, at any rate.

'I wouldn't ask any more questions if I were you,' I said, before she did.

'I'll see if he's free.'

I turned away so I could grimace a little while my stomach convulsed mildly, lighting a chain of pain that flashed across my body in a dozen different places. She retreated to her poky little office and I saw her pick up the phone through the frosted glass. When she came out she waved me on.

'You're very lucky. It's Saturday today; he's not often in.'

'Am I? Is it? Where is he when he is in, these days?'

'Floor four, end of the corridor.' Her tone hadn't got any more welcoming, but I was through.

Funny how a well-timed line can slant things for you, or how just the slightest gimmick can turn the odds, whether it be women or work or whatever. It tortured me when I was a young man, knowing that a few phrases and expressions in the right places at the right time could open up a new pair of legs or a new job. That was all it was, like knowing the combination for a safe. Every situation could be unlocked, and every chancer knows it. It was a pity I only ever got the numbers for the cheapest tricks.

Four floors up, eight flights of unyielding stairs, and me barely able to cover nine yards on the flat without having to stop and lean on something or other. I waited in the corridor to get my breath back but it didn't come. It looked like I'd have to go in gasping, gasping and shameless.

I wasn't the only one to get my own office, or have my name on the door. His was spelt out in bright brass lettering. It was on his desk too: I didn't bother to knock. He knew I was coming.

'Llywelyn,' he said, sitting behind this big wooden desk like he was about to read the nine o'clock news. 'What the bloody hell do you want?'

He hadn't changed much. A few grey streaks, maybe the jaw line had softened a little, that was all. The bastard looked distinguished, and I looked like death warmed up. Death with a few surplus pounds around the middle.

'Hello, Doc.'

'Well?' he said, bluntly. He made no comment on my appearance.

'Well. How are you?'

'Out with it.'

'How's Carol?' I asked, without being aware my mouth was even moving. By the time I'd finished speaking I was already in despair. It's like giving up cigarettes – you can stop successfully for years and then light up one day without even thinking about it and be back in the rut, instantly.

Richard's hostility was dampened. It was not, he knew, what I'd come for, but it had a lot of weight behind it. It was a question to which he could not deny me an answer. He was the only person in the world I talked to about this, who I could talk to, and he had never refused me before. I'd promised myself to stop asking questions from the start, when it was fairly obvious it was going to be a memory I could no longer carry, except however heavy the load you can never forget, and he knew this.

I have cut off so much of my life. Every time it went wrong I turned around, and for most of my existence I have been conceived anew each morning, a fully grown man in an unmade bed, which is not that unusual for men of my age. Except it doesn't leave you much room to manoeuvre, not with so much in wait supposedly forgotten. Even if you convince yourself otherwise, they remain out there, the hooks and snags and claims of the past, ready to trip you up and remind you that things are unchanged. That things are sorely messed up, and that it's too late for you to do anything about it.

'You're interested in Carol again, are you?' he said, resignedly.

I couldn't remember the last time I'd asked him about Carol (one January evening outside a steakhouse by the Hippodrome. See what I mean?). Other people may have perceived that silence as indifference, and silence was all you'd get out of me on the subject, but Richard was the only person around who knew me well enough to know differently. The world is not that big a place, and all of us lone figures you see dotted about the place, at the bar or in the launderette, we have those who we have left behind or who have left us.

Suffice to say I didn't mean for things to work out like this. The phone calls I never made, the cheques I never sent, the visits I never paid: somehow the money or the courage was always wanting, and of course the longer you leave these things the harder it becomes to do them. So we hadn't met or spoken once since the day I ran scared shitless from that town of mine with my tail between my legs, fleeing my sweet responsibilities with a knee-jerk retreat. I was not, nor will I ever be, ready to become a father. There was no way a man like me could guide a little one through the world I knew, and everything that has passed since then is evidence of that. The drink and meanness and cheap fear, the hollow nights and stupid days and great, gulping years, all this plainly shows you so. In the darker moments, when I am unhinged and unaware, a voice catches me and

241

tells me that was the way I wanted it, but I don't listen. I don't listen to that kind of crap.

From what I'd heard about her end there was nothing to contradict the notion they were both better off without me, nothing to disprove the hastily scrawled note thrust into my hands during the moments prior to departure saying she thought it for the best, after all. She found somebody else soon enough, which could hardly have been much of a challenge, and that certainly seemed to be that. The CSA never asked me for any money. I did ring her once, years ago, late one night. She said hello and I hung up: it was enough. Those two soft syllables and the quiet sound of her breathing were more than I could handle. Amazing to relate, I was young, I was too young once.

'You know I'm always interested,' I said. 'Seen her recently?'

'No. She died. She divorced that producer from Cardiff, and pretty soon after she found out she had throat cancer. She went last spring, I think.' He said it as if he were talking about the weather, and I think he meant to come across like that, seeing how pissed off he seemed to be with me. Very faintly a wire snapped somewhere. Something descended that was very heavy and gentle at the same time, like a large snowfall, and I felt it tight across my chest.

'I see.'

'Perhaps you can stop pretending you'll make things up with her now.'

'I don't know, being dead doesn't reduce the odds that much.'

I laughed a little, or at least I tried. I didn't ask about our son. I had never been able to do it, except once, in the early days before the slide was so obvious, to ask about the colour of his eyes.

'If it's any consolation, she's always been intelligent enough to know that,' said Dr Jenkins.

It did the trick: all right, I thought, that's enough of that. Some things are better left undiscussed, whatever therapists or telephone companies will have you believe. Not that I didn't try, in some pub rarely visited when closing time rolled around, a few whisky confessions to a drunk and equally troubled stranger. And I was always forgiven, whenever I bowed my sagging head, by my brother irredeemables. It was about as comforting as a night on a park bench, but you wouldn't want to bother better folk with it. To be seen as a man of dignity you have to hold your tongue and swallow your shame, if you would walk with people who value such things. Instead I switched to the matter at hand and exposed another part of myself. It was only Rich Jenkins. Not much of an old boys' network, but then I wasn't much of an old boy.

'OK Doc,' I said. I'd always called him Doc, ever since he was a medical student (at Cambridge, no less). 'I took this job on and I'm a tad out of my depth. I think I'm being outflanked, so to speak, and it's important I'm in working health. I got lairy with someone last night and it flipped back in my face. I took a pretty bad beating, as you can probably see.' So far so good, I thought, but the next part was the most difficult. I realized I hadn't looked him in the eye since I came in, and I knew that I couldn't. My hands were still shaking. I hid them in my pockets.

'Also, the drinking seems to have got a little out of control.' I was making my excuses to the window; the city skyline and my own pale reflection. 'I thought it was all right, but what with the pressure and so on, I've been overdoing it. I feel like death and this time I'm too scared to drink it off. Well, to be accurate, I don't have the money or the time. Anyway, I need treatment. I need to be in better shape than this and soon, otherwise I'm in the shit.'

'You're never in the shit,' said Dr Jenkins, finally, after an awesome silence. I don't think he was looking at me either, but then I wasn't in a position to tell. 'You get by. You chance it and you fumble on. That's what you do: you look after yourself, and everyone else be damned. Don't you worry, you're not going to sink any deeper than you are already. I simply can't believe that's possible.'

'I appreciate your concern,' I said, pleased to find a kernel of anger coming into bud somewhere inside myself. It's nice to find something in there in these moments. 'But it wasn't the way I planned it, you know, not at all. Did you think I'd end up like this?'

'Frankly, yes, and I don't care. I'm not going to pull you out any more. Bite the bullet and ride it out. What do you take me for? In the past, what, five years, you've never seen me once except to drift in here stinking like a brewery, expecting me to put you back on the tracks as if you were a toy train, and for what? When was the last time you ever did anything for me, or anybody else?'

'What did you want me to do? Perhaps we could go to your club and play a few rounds of golf. Or why don't I come over some time, with a bottle of wine or five, so you can introduce me to your lovely family? Or perhaps you'd like to come over the river and sample the delights of Bedminster. Failing that, maybe I could pull in some debts for you, or spy on your wife. Be honest: you wouldn't trust me to mow your lawn, would you?'

'No,' he said. 'I wouldn't. You're no good to anybody. At first I could believe you'd just fallen in with a bad crowd, but that's impossible these days. I know all about it, you and Bruce and those drugs. What happened to it, exactly, all that money? Did you have to buy your way out, when they got you? I've always wondered.'

'There wasn't any money,' I said. It was telling, in retrospect, that I took no offence at this, that I thought it was a natural conclusion for him to jump to. 'It was just a favour I did for him. I didn't know what I was doing. Doc, I mean, I didn't want to know, it was just a favour owed. I stayed out as far as I could. I could hardly refuse, considering what he'd done for me. In my line of work it's important to maintain good relations with the police.'

'Jesus Christ.' Rich waited for me to say something but my mouth was as dry as a tomb, my mind frozen like it is every time it strays too close to an old truth. 'What did Bruce ever do for you?'

'Bruce was the one who got me the job.'

'Great, I remember it well. I remember you telling me, all full of yourself, head crammed with old films, swaggering about in a trench coat handing out cheap business cards at every opportunity. God only knows what they all thought of you. If that's the only favour the police ever did you it wasn't much, was it?'

'I got some good cases from them, at the beginning, until that business with Bruce came out. They couldn't very well associate with me after that.'

'Why not? Knight's as bad as Bruce. They're all a bunch of crooks, you know, your uniformed acquaintances. I do have contact with these people; I've known some of them for longer than you have.'

He was right, of course, I can admit that now. Why I felt so indebted to Bruce I find hard to explain. Perhaps it was nice to think there was somebody I could actually pay back, I don't know. I don't even know, now, if I ever owed him anything in the first place, but there is an understandable temptation to tell yourself that, hey, here is somebody whose help you can return when your seedy life story is swollen with those whose help you cannot, whose trust you have broken, who you have failed and continue to fail. Especially when there are even more who have never helped you at all: in retrospect the quality and quantity of the favours done for me in this life are not that high, on average, though I may be too ungrateful to know about them all. But I can remember wanting badly to be a good man once.

'It's no exaggeration,' he went on. 'They tried to get Knight years ago, and the only reason he wasn't drummed out or slapped behind bars was because he could hang it all on somebody else, somebody who wasn't able to answer back, seeing he was in several pieces.'

'Bruce,' I mumbled. 'In that car bomb.'

'No one ever admitted responsibility for that, you know, the IRA or the INLA or the Derry Boy Scouts.'

'You're saying?' I asked, at a loss again.

'Nothing more than that, Llywelyn, nothing more than that. Not one paramilitary group has claimed it as their own, this act of supposed terrorism that proved so fortuitous for your good friend Knight.'

'Oh, come on, Jenks,' I said, bemused now. 'That's a step too far. The man's not a murderer.' But we both knew he was, either way you looked at it, O'Connell or Bruce or both, and I caught the lie too late to stop it.

He sighed. 'Well, you're probably right. Still, you never know where you are with that crowd.'

'No. I'm sure they skim a bit here and there now and again. It's inevitable really, if you think about the nature of their job. You could hardly expect them to be whiter than white with a workload like they've got. Maybe it's the only way a police force can work.'

'Yeah.' He nodded, the pair of us slowly convincing ourselves for our own sakes; oh yeah. It's funny how when it comes to the people you know there is this tendency to apologize for the swine and knock the saints. Whatever it takes to bring the bastards up, and the nice guys down, to your own level. Anything, as long as you don't have to change.

Take McKellan: for years I hated that man, almost as much as he hated me. It wasn't that he was censorious, or joyless, or distant and disdainful and almost constantly abrasive, he was all these things, but the reason I hated him was because I thought he had no right to be. I objected to this air of tired, deliberate self-righteousness he insisted on carrying around with him. The mishandled proverbs, the tutting and sighing and pointed looks, the jobs he wouldn't let me handle or even let me near, all withheld with a dismissive snort and a homily he'd heard on *Songs of Praise*: even when you could laugh at him it got on your tits. I mean, it was life-draining. He wasn't a great poster boy for always doing the right thing, the miserable old sod. And a man as ridiculously upright as that, especially one in this profession, surely couldn't be as straight as he seemed. Maybe he wasn't, but it took several struggling, increasingly dirty years on my own before I could concede that he was certainly straighter than I.

I looked at Rich, lost also in thoughts of his own, much calmer now that we had talked a little. The room was so quiet you could hear the rain patter softly on the window. My hands still shook unobserved in their pockets. I was going to say something but he spoke first:

'I was glad, you know, when they turned on you like that, when they revoked your membership of their little gang,' he said, putting both his hands on his desk like a judge delivering a verdict. 'I thought it was for the best.'

'What do you think it is now?' I said. 'Fucking look at me!' I went to wipe a thread of spittle from the corner of my mouth but it was my broken hand, and I succeeded only in rolling it to the underside of my jaw. That vein was tapping out a salsa beat in the corner of my forehead, but the good doctor remained dead calm, placid in the black leather of his expensive executive chair.

'It could have been a lot worse if it'd gone on longer,' he said. 'Knight's under investigation himself now, and it's about bloody time. Some councillor's up in arms about tacit police cooperation with local dealers, blind-eye backhanders, something like that – I heard it from one of my solicitor friends. It's not in the papers yet but anyone could tell you. The fucking Citizens Advice Bureau in this town could tell you. You must—'

'I don't want to know,' I said, and I didn't. 'Are you going to fix me up or not?' If it came to it I could take my chances with half a dozen aspirins and hope for the best.

'You never did, did you?' he said, not in a pointed way, just thoughtfully, and tilted his head. Appraising something, I thought, looking for any vestige of the days when we were friends and the world was a different place, way back when my morals were fine and life hadn't started its awkward habit of shifting the goalposts. Measuring the differences that had grown between us, all the chasms and crevices we were too polite or merely too evasive to mention. This is what I like to think he was thinking.

'All right,' he said. 'But I have to warn you, my prices have gone up a bit.'

Dr Jenkins's prices had gone up two hundred per cent. He had more to lose now, he argued, with two children in private school and the possibility of making consultant next year, and so he charged more.

'I had a young solicitor in here last year, a heroin addict who didn't want to go on the register,' he offered, by way of an explanation. 'Wanted some methadone so he could ease himself off. Quite insistent. Now if you go back on to heroin while taking methadone it'll probably kill you. Would you want to take the responsibility for that, with someone that young? He was still on his training contract, I think. Had him in here every other week for his dose.'

'What happened?'

'Oh, he moved away, thank God,' he said, perhaps a little too quickly. 'But I've learnt my lesson: I've priced myself out of the market. The only patients I want to deal with now are the dead ones, the ones they find in the street and wheel in on trolleys.'

He had more to lose than me, I'll give him that. He was worth it too. He'd been on sabbatical one time, or over-extended holiday, and this GP had jabbed me with some chemical deterrent that makes you throw up if you so much as sniff the barmaid's apron. Turns everything into meths. I had never vomited so much in my life.

'Don't worry,' I said. 'This'll be the last time I bother you, I swear,' What I had to swear by I couldn't say.

'Oh, I've heard that before,' he said, but it was true enough. It was the last time he would see me or my problems, and I don't think either of us minded much. We'd been wanting to wrap it up for years. I paid him with a cheque of the purest rubber and rolled up my arm expectantly.

'Did they cremate her or bury her?' I asked.

'Why, going to pine longingly by the graveside?' He laughed, and I turned red, although you wouldn't have noticed, not with a mush like mine.

'You know what your problem is, don't you?' he asked, rhetorically. He was always in the habit of creating some diversion as the plunger sank into the pierced flesh. 'You're an idiot.'

Then I was bouncing down those stone steps in a discernibly jaunty manner and out on to St Michael's Mount, winding all the way down to the depths of the town, following its well-worn course like water. My hands were steady now. A few pills of this, that and the other and a shot in the arm. I always made a point of not asking what I was getting and he knew there was no point in telling me. I felt better as soon as he told me I would.

That was it, along with a few tut-tuts and something about long-term damage. All in one ear and out the other, as per, except this time it was almost excusable because there was enough to worry about already. There was enough riding on the next fourteen or fifteen hours alone, and the closest I'd come to positive action was to flirt idly with the idea of jumping off a bridge. But there were no plans left.

In the boot of my rented Rover, in the visitor's car park of a hospital that no one ever visited, there was seven grand's worth of electronics. If I was lucky I could get a few hundred for it down the pawn shop. I didn't know anybody who was worth anything any more. The gear was too specialized for me. I have learnt only the lowliest tricks. A life spent trawling the ugliest pubs and shadiest streets like a pilgrim, and nothing to show for it but bar-room wisdom and half a dozen anecdotes not worth the telling. Meanwhile a woman not one hundred miles away married someone else (twice) and died alone.

I got a flashback of a cartoon I used to watch as a child; this coyote who kept running off clifftops at leg-blurring speed. Once he looked down and saw where he was he plummeted like an anvil. Already I had this light-footed sensation and it was not a pleasurable feeling. I have gone too far, I thought, and the only thing to do is keep going and not look anywhere at all.

I cadged a cigarette off a doctor smoking around the fire exit. The sight of him puffing away cheered me up a bit for some reason. Then I got in the car, and it felt like two or three people got in with me who I could not see and would not ever see again.

CHAPTER 3

I t wasn't house policy at Delia's place of work to hand out home telephone numbers. If they ever made an exception to this admittedly sensible rule it wasn't going to be for somebody who looked like me, and bribing people with cheques is harder than getting pissed on Baileys, so all I did was jabber angrily in what I thought were eloquent and compassionate tones. It always caught me by surprise, the headlong rush of my medicine. Sedation is my home territory, the gentle pint-by-pint erosion of the universe on a nightly basis, and this treatment was more like the big bang. I wonder whether anyone ever got used to it, or did the booze always get to them first?

'We can try ringing her later, if you like, and pass on your message,' one of them said, for about the fourth or fifth time. It was difficult to believe this without handing over some of the folding as a gesture of goodwill, and all I had was spare change. I actually took it out to count, like some fuddled but benevolent uncle among nieces, happily ignorant of the rate of inflation. Then somebody told me they didn't have a payphone and I got the better of myself.

'All right, but it's very important. Tell her to be at the bar at seven, like we discussed. Make sure she knows.' I repeated this until they offered me a pen and paper so I could write it down, and then they skilfully ushered me out with much hard-won experience. The whole thing was probably unnecessary, but I was worried and I needed reassurance, and of course I didn't get any.

In the street, shortly after my courteous ejection, it wasn't long before I started getting self-conscious. It was still a bit early for the knocking shops and I was the only punter about; a woman with a two-wheeled shopping trolley had to swerve around me as I stood flicking the last of the doorway's taffeta strands off my shoulder.

'Don't forget,' I yelled, and shuffled away. There couldn't have been more than five or six people in sight but they were all looking at me. Now you don't want to start feeling conspicuous on the stuff I was on, not if you're under pressure in the first place. For some reason it accentuates all these kinds of feelings, and amplifies them. By the time I'd reached the end of Old Market Street there was an unmarked Mondeo in the corner of my eye no matter where I looked, and the scant hours left were turning into minutes, seconds, moments: they had shrunk so small they could fly by in the blink of an eye. It may have been needed, this druggy paranoiac whooshing of time, in order for me to get off my arse, but it was no good for the nerves.

I still didn't have any way to record sound, and if they wanted audio they'd better have it. They'd better have anything they wanted, so I took the car around to Broadmead but the car parks around there are all manned and I didn't want to part with what cash I had left. In a flash of inspiration I took it round the back of John Lewis's and left it in the loading bay, knowing I wasn't likely to dilly-dally. I am not the sort of man to be distracted by a nice pair of trousers or a cheap wok and there are no pubs in the middle of Broadmead. I got a long-play tape recorder at Tandy's and seeing I couldn't really afford any of it I threw in a radial microphone too. At the loading bay a man with a lorry full of mattresses was trying to get the shop staff to carry them across the yard, and I could still see them at each other's throats in my rear-view when I drove their only obstacle out of the way.

The doorman at the Hilton had no top hat, and I wondered what had happened to it. Perhaps this guy was just too uncouth for headwear, because when I approached he stepped out to put a gloved hand on the bonnet, and I think I was about to get some cursory directions to the nearest YMCA until I waved my room keys about. He took a little step back, as if a passing dog had commented on the weather, and I was through.

The stairs from the car park came up on the other side of reception, so I didn't have to run that particular gauntlet, but I still clutched my keys like a talisman. I've never liked to let go of a set of keys, and somewhere in the flat there was a set for every place I've ever rented. Perhaps there is something symbolic in this, or perhaps it's just sheer kleptomania. There were surely few practical advantages in either case, but I was glad I had my keys with me now. There must be plenty of people who'd stop to ask what someone of my appearance was doing roaming the Hilton unaccompanied, carrying what seemed to be a smoke alarm and trailing electrical cables. But it was early afternoon, and I made it to the room unassisted and unmolested.

The key worked fine, but I wasn't sure I was in the right place at first. I suppose I expected stains on the sheets and empty bottles on the window sill, but of course it had all gone and the room's travesty counter had been reset to zero once more, ready for the entire act to occur all over again. I had forgotten about cleaning maids, forgotten or ceased to believe that such an animal existed. Who knows how many transgressions these women wiped away, what awful secrets they bundled up and ferried off to laundry? Maybe only they can speak of all that goes on in these innocuous, replicated rooms, much, much more than this, I'm sure. I stopped believing in the universe's secret moral scoreboard a long time ago, but I have searched for it in far more unusual places than the laundry room of the St Mary Redcliffe Hilton, and I was pleased to think somebody somewhere might be keeping some kind of count.

I peeled the cellophane off the sticky-backed plastic and stuck the camera on the ceiling squarely over the centre of the bed. Now the room had two smoke alarms, but I doubt he would notice a thing like that by the time he was in here, nor would he probably mind too much about the pair of muddy man-sized footprints on the sheets. For all their powers, as impressive as they were, I doubt the maids had really made things any easier for me. Although to be fair they'd made it easy to pretend nothing had happened yet, to pretend that this was the first time I'd ever been here, and for that I was grateful. You don't need that kind of distraction.

I lifted the valance but the bed was a simple divan, and I had to tear through the fabric with my bare hands – hand, rather – to make a space for the tape recorder and microphone. Then I tucked the power cable in along the edges until it reached the bedside table, unplugged the radio-alarm, and hooked it up. I'd have to nip in here an hour or two beforehand to turn it all on but as long as I kept my wits about me it would be all right. Then I stepped back and surveyed my handiwork. It was a load of bollocks really, a complete improvisation, but Delia was a good-looking girl and that was what mattered.

There wasn't anything else to do now but wait. If Knight or anybody else bothered me I could tell them everything was in place, and I thought about a pint in the White Hart before remembering I'd better not set foot in there again. There was the Reckless Engineer, just down by the station, but when I thought about it a bit more I decided I'd better not set foot in any pub whatsoever until six or so at the earliest. The rope had gone slack for a couple of hours and the best idea I could come up with before hanging myself with it was to drive the car somewhere, or just anywhere, so I ambled downstairs again.

While I was fixing up the camera, unless I hadn't noticed it on the way in, somebody in the lobby had put up a board on a wooden trestle. It was covered in maroon felt and had a load of gold plastic letters on it that read, more or less in a straight line: 'Bristol City Council Annual Business Initiative – The Defoe Room 7.30 p.m.'. So that's the conference she told me about, I thought, another opportunity for Dixon and the other captains of industry to drink free champagne and slip a few backhanders to the local council, or vice versa. Then I went on down to the car, and before I left I took the receiver out of the boot and opened it up, watching the tiny LCD screen slide out on its little runners, showing me that bland little honeytrap in miniature, in all its grainy monochrome glory. I slid the blank cassette into the video machine. Six hours of recording time, it had. I'd be surprised if he got it over with quicker than me, but six hours, surely, was excessive. Then I put the case back and absently turned the ignition, faintly bemused that everything seemed to be in order, and took the car out into the street. Then, somewhere around Redlands a good twenty minutes later, I remembered about the councillor Richard Jenkins had told me was making allegations of police corruption against David Knight and his officers, who was calling for an investigation. Then I remembered how Knight had a black Honda Civic like the one Dixon was supposed to have had – Dixon, who might not be a captain of industry at all. Then I stopped at a lay-by that had a phone box, and tried to think about exactly what I would say.

'Mrs Dixon here,' went the voice.

'No it isn't,' I said. 'Dave Knight and I had a good long talk this morning. Finally. I don't think you were planning on that happening, were you?'

There was no answer.

'I suppose you wanted to keep my fee for yourself. Don't blame you, I gave you a ridiculous quote. But then you never intended to pay me, did you? Just get some leverage on me and then pocket however much Knight and your colleagues gave you to get the job done. I don't think Dave is too pleased with your plan of action. Has he had a little chat with you yet? He can be awfully persuasive, can't he? You know, if you didn't want me to think you were a policewoman you shouldn't drive about the place in a white Mondeo.'

'Why are you ringing me?' she asked, and her voice wavered noticeably. Point made, I thought, but there was something else I had to know.

'Just to let you know that you're in the shit. It gives me some satisfaction, you know. Because I didn't appreciate the rape threat, and neither did Dave, who'd never risk his reputation backing up a transparent set-up, even if it hadn't been a plan to skim some extra on the side for yourself. So your bluff is called. Dave and I go way back: you should keep that in mind. In fact, we go back all the way to O'Connell.'

I didn't have to wait long:

'Who?' she said, and then the pips went and I was down to coppers. It was enough. I hadn't read anything in the papers about a body being found recently. This woman was a newcomer, with no idea who he was, and if she and Knight were trying to gag someone it had nothing to do with O'Connell. More likely it was linked to Dave Knight's ability to buy a Civic for cash on an inspector's salary, and that in turn probably involved something along the old lines of suitcases that shouldn't be opened and ill-looking men with sunken eyes. It was still going on.

All this from one short phone call. People go on about the stupidity of the police, about the fucked-up idiocy of the filth, but I guess it's a blessing as well as a curse. I don't think it's even true stupidity, not as you might know it, but the tendency to make a certain kind of mistake, the kinds of mistakes that are made by people who have too much on the line. I had nothing, and that was my sole advantage.

I put the receiver back on its cradle and stepped out of the box, watching a passenger jet from the airport on the other side of town veer east. Short-haul to Paris maybe, or Madrid. I had never been to either of those places, and now I never would. I wasn't too sure exactly what I would do now, except the one thing I'd been needing to do for days. I took the Rover round to the basement level of a multi-storey near Clifton Triangle, where there was no light, put the seat down and slept. I slept like a baby, and dreamt of nothing; nothing I could remember, anyway. I hadn't slept like that for a long time, soundly, sober, and free of doubt. Don't ask me how I did it.

The Saturday shopping crowd came and went, slamming down car boots full of stuff I didn't have, bumping trolleys and shepherding children. I slept through it all. The sun slipped behind the roof line. The pubs began to open their doors to the weekend warriors, fighting for their lives against the company clock, and slowly the place emptied of life. Then, once I was alone again, I awoke, as I knew I would.

I had thought myself a cynical man. Now I knew I wasn't. It was the blind faith of a zealot which punched the gear lever into reverse, which turned the ignition, which flipped the dipped headlights into their alien orange glow. It was nothing but sheer hope which sent the car up and out and on its way to the conclusion ahead. A man with any sense, if he'd got involved in the first place, would have gone back to sleep. He would have leant back, closed his eyes and let it all catch up with him, as it inevitably would. But not me.

I was lost, and I could have told you that and meant it, but I still kept my foot on the accelerator. I still sent the car through Park Row and Perry Road like a joyrider. I hung a right down Colston Street and followed the one-way system around St Augustine's Parade like a leaf on a stream, bolting down Baldwin Street and Bristol Bridge as if I were running on rails, just footsteps away from where Bruce was blown to pieces all those years ago, and the lights were green all the way. All the fucking way, every bloody sodding one, and after I'd stopped skimming across the city like a flat stone over water and the dull, mirror-glassed Hilton squatted ahead, the car bumped down the basement ramp as easily as a coin down a slot. The barrier was fixed in the up position with not a doorman in sight, not even a top hat left lying at the kerbside. I didn't know what it meant, exactly, but I knew it meant something.

CHAPTER 4

It had been my intention to get to the Hilton before Delia so I could catch her on the way in, put her on my arm to fend off any questions about my admission, and sneak into the hotel bar. Expecting her to arrive on foot, I walked back up the ramp and past the barrier to the pavement, only to see her sail past me two minutes later in a brand-new Golf. It paid the bills, I grant you, fucking strange men. I saw that there was a baby seat on the passenger side and a few harried-looking soft toys in the foot well and decided, just for the hell of it, that Knight's female friend had never persuaded her to report me for sexual assault at all. It was just possible, I suppose, that it was another part of her bluff. Then I put the whole thing out of my mind and kept it there.

'You don't look too good, Robin,' she said when she got out, smoothing down the front of a black dress that ran to just above her knees. She had on a pair of delicate, pointy-looking boots that covered most of her calves and, I noticed, she had dyed her hair black. It suited her.

'No,' I agreed, 'I had the shit beaten out of me. Shall we go in?'

She wasn't a tall girl but I managed to crouch behind her as we skirted awkwardly past the receptionist and concierge and glass collectors and whatever lackeys and flunkeys these places have floating about, and nobody seemed to notice. The bar was already quite busy with the sort of clientele you might expect, and I thought I added a bit of colour, to be honest with you, but I don't think many of those people would have seen it that way. It didn't worry me, not once the bar was in sight, and then I swear I was as giddy as a schoolboy, walking on air across the velvet carpet and barely able to feel my own legs moving. It was all I could do to stop myself downing drinks off the nearest table, and when I finally got there I almost ordered a jugful of the top shelf straight off.

Instead I nudged myself into the corner, right up against the wood panelling, trying to make myself as unobtrusive as possible. It gave me a good view of the whole room, but that wasn't something I cared about right then. Delia sat down one stool away, not wanting to associate with me too obviously, perhaps because she didn't want to give the game away, or perhaps because the prospect of booze had already cast its drooling glaze across my face.

'A pint, please,' I said, with some restraint, to the figure in the waistcoat.

'A pint of what?'

I hadn't even read the names on the pumps.

'Oh, the usual,' I said, tripping over my words, not even thinking what I was saying. 'You pick it. Room sixty-five, name's Dixon.'

That one disappeared in the time it took to pour, although it had a strange metallic tang, from the medicine I expect, and I started lining them up. One day soon the bar would close for ever. I was too preoccupied to notice much during the first two or three and then I looked up to see Delia nibbling at another one of those cocktails that looked like a burst blood vessel in a glass, trying to catch my attention by tapping her painted fingernails on the marble counter.

'I don't know what he looks like,' she said.

'Don't worry, I'll point him out.'

'Is he with the conference?'

'Yeah.'

'What if he doesn't come into the bar?'

'Then we're in a spot of bother,' I said, and left it at that, raising a glass and not putting it down until I knew she wasn't going to ask any more questions. I don't think she thought she was going to get much sense out of me anyway. Then she pulled a book out of her handbag, a Penguin Classic it looked like, and starting reading it right at the bar.

I had a good look at her, seeing it would be the last time. She clearly didn't have any idea I knew about the arrangement she'd made with Mrs Dixon, Mrs whoever-she-was, or she wouldn't have been sitting there like that. I'd like to think I could inspire a little fear, even if only in a woman. I stared openly at her, once she had her head safely tucked in her book, and tried to think about it. About damp plaster, old sweat, shitting in a pot you kept under your bed, iodine in your food, showers with other men, hatred, navy denims, once-a-week visiting hours without visitors, cramped rooms where the lights got turned on and off by someone else; all that she had conspired to offer me. It was hard, though, to sit at a free bar in the Hilton next to a young beautiful woman and keep your mind on all that.

'How's your kid?' I said. 'How's your kid doing?'

Delia looked at me in a strange way and said, very slowly:

'All right.'

Fair enough, I thought. It wasn't exactly the time or the place for a friendly chat about the trials and tribulations of motherhood. I had another drink, Delia turned a few pages. I didn't feel much suspense, or nervousness; life proceeded as normal and time neither speeded up nor slowed down. Everything was laid out, if not thought out, and I felt I was equal to what lay ahead. It was quite pleasant, really.

The next phase began when the double doors in the side wall swung ceremoniously open, and a conference-load of businessmen and council-lors nodded and murmured their way into the bar. Delia twirled around expectantly, saw that my face was still searching, and went back to her book. I recognized him, just like he looked in the photo, but in an olive jacket with an open-necked shirt and a pair of chinos. A liberal, I assumed: even I wore a suit, although a track-suit would have looked smarter, if it was clean. I turned my back on them and described him to her. She cast a quick glance in his direc-tion and then said something that made me laugh:

'What shall we do?' she said. I told her to wait till he came to the bar and she moved a little farther away, as if my aura were an impediment to seduction, which it probably was. For the first two rounds some other guy from his group came up to get the drinks, and Delia began to look a little restless, but the third time round he made the trip himself and they struck up a conversa-tion. I couldn't hear what they were saying but I think it was something about the book, which was coming in very useful for Delia that night. He didn't look much, about five seven, maybe, and slim. I heard him order the drinks and his voice was boyish, and a bit smarmy. I expected more, I suppose, considering what he was trying to take on.

He went off to take his friends their drinks but he came back, and shortly after this the pair of them moved off to a table of their own. It was all up to him now, and I watched keenly, although I knew how it would end. The result was always the same, but I rooted for him anyway. The thing was, with this guy, he didn't really make it a spectator sport. The build-up wasn't one of those flirty, touchy-feely affairs at all; the two of them just nattered on and on for ages, and even with so much riding on it my attention span was well overrun.

Pints came and went. I noticed nothing; bugger all. The roof could have fallen in for all I cared. All I felt was the cool of the glass and the sparkle at the back of my throat, growing slowly over my body, right down to the steadying pit of my stomach. Then, soon after, my veins opening like eyes, my mind reappearing like an old friend. I was beginning to feel myself again, whoever that was. Half pissed in no time with nobody so much as cocking an eyelid, not that I saw. I wasn't seeing very much at all: equilibrium had been achieved.

'Bugger me,' I said to myself as I picked up another drink. My crippled, clenched hand fitted the circumference of a pint glass exactly. It seemed almost like evolution. 'Look at that,' I said to nobody in particular. As soon I realized I was talking to myself I swung around, looking for someone I could talk to before I launched into a monologue, someone I could talk to about anything at all, but the drinkers in these posh hotels don't tend to indulge you.

'He's gone to the toilet,' somebody near me said,

and I thought: that has to be a euphemism of some kind, cheeky sod, and then I saw that it was Delia.

'Oh. Right. Going OK, is it? It doesn't usually take this much time.'

'Fine. We've covered politics and literature, so I don't think it'll take much longer. Can I have the room key?'

'Oh shit. Yeah, of course,' I said, and handed it to her, although she wouldn't need it. I would make sure of that. It was just that I was rooting for him, and I wanted to see him come through.

'Going OK, is it?'

'You just asked me that.'

'Sorry. You know, Delia, I wasn't going to say it but now you've dyed your hair black you really do remind me of a girl I used to know, back, oh, a lifetime ago.' But she was scurrying back to the table before he could return, and she didn't hear, or she chose to ignore me. Which would have been understandable.

Right, I thought, this is it: you'd better stay sharp from here on in. Pay attention. Better move on to the bottled lagers, if you have to have something, because they're smaller and they always seem to take just as long to drink. This is the problem with reaching equilibrium: as you get older it keeps moving one drink farther down the line, and by the time you reach it you've built up such a head of steam you can't help but overshoot. Then you're just fucking pissed.

Gently, so as not to slip off the stool, I turned my torso the forty or fifty degrees necessary to slide the lovebirds into view and rested an elbow on the bar for support. The room was bustling and my vision was ever so slightly blurred, so I didn't expect to clap eyes on them straight away, but I peered unashamedly into the crowd, its faces swimming in and out of focus, each one careful to be found looking in some other direction, and came up dry. After a couple of unsuccessful sweeps I started to experience my first palpitations of the evening. Then, mercifully, a bunch of German women relocated to an emptying table and unwittingly prevented heart seizure by opening up a new field of vision.

The body nestling in that big square leather chair was unmistakable. Her face was nicely uplit by an over-sized lampshade on a nearby table and her slender legs were crossed at the knee. Opposite her was your man Dixon, still holding back from making any public display, face inclined in an interested but paternal manner, his roving hands holding firmly on to the arms of his chair. Nothing to indicate he was fighting a losing battle at all, except he couldn't take his eyes off her. I'd seen it all enough times to know that this was a foregone conclusion. She was right: they'd be heading upstairs any time now. He had already reached out to touch her leg once or twice, ostensibly to emphasize something he was saying, and with a man of that type once contact is finally made the rest of it follows on fast.

Bugger it, I thought, although I wasn't really surprised. Just because I am adept at hiding myself from the inevitable, it doesn't necessarily mean I always forget that it's there. Seeing how it was all going to kick off within a few minutes, and I was still at least two steps safely removed from being blind drunk, I ordered one of the cheaper Scotches. Couldn't hurt, could it? I brought it up through my nose, but the tumbler fell safely on to the thick carpet. Another couple of inches to the right and it would have landed on the tiles around the foot of the bar and smashed into pieces. Evidently still a little under the weather, medicine or no. Somebody near me asks whether I'm all right, which I take to be a coded message for please piss off, and everybody else pretends I'm not there. But Dixon and Delia have already left the room.

The sacred institution of marriage: not that hard to take it down a peg or two. Even I could knock it into a cocked hat, me of all people, with a few grand's worth of Jeremy Beadle technology and a little rented flesh. I wondered whether he had much to lose, and whether he would have lost it had she known. You'd think so, knowing how much Knight was relying on us. Perhaps he loved her, his real wife, or perhaps she was wealthy, or it was all he wanted, to live his little detached four-bedroomed family life. There was plenty of it about, I'd seen it glowing dully at me from behind countless net curtains in streets all over town. It couldn't take much, or be a lot to ask for. I might have considered his political career, but I would have thought you're on safe ground these days as long as you don't bugger your grandchildren.

On first impressions I didn't care for him parti-cularly, I have to say, no more than any other random punter. I wasn't out to do him any favours. It was just there were so few things left I could do, and this was one of them. Like the floored man sending a final fist into the groin of his assailant before the flurry of kicks came, striking out one last time before folding into the foetal position, before darkness descends: fuck them, fuck it all. I heaved my gut off the stool and found my unsteady feet. The room had the soft oscill-ation of a cross-Channel ferry. It didn't stop me from making the lifts in time to stick a muddied shoe between the closing doors, very likely putting stop to plans for an imminent embrace of one-sided passion.

Timing was a key issue here. An important factor was that if I'd warned him off any earlier he prob-ably wouldn't have believed he'd ever do this sort of thing in the first place. From what I knew of the guy, or what I could perceive, he fancied himself as a bit of an upstanding citizen, and I imagine it would be an uphill struggle convincing your average holier-than-thou personality he's in danger of committing adultery with a prostitute unless he's already most of the way there. Another consideration, no less serious, was that Knight or Gilboursen could have decided to drop by and check up at any point beforehand. My key motive, though, if we're to be frank, was that I wanted to see whether he'd fall for it. But he was just the same as the rest of them. In any case, it's typical of me to leave the things that really matter till the last minute.

Dixon looked at me warily, though not in the eye, and Delia reflexively took a step backwards, not that there was anywhere she could have run to in a closed lift. Then, for the first time, and in a far from elegant frame of mind, I had to think how I'd actually put the message across. There was only one sure way to do it, I felt: threaten the guy. Come across hard and scare him into perspective.

'You'd better leave that girl alone, Dixon.'

Dixon wasn't at all curious about how I'd come to know his name. I thought it might establish my credentials, so to speak, but perhaps he had a high enough political profile for all sorts of people to know his name already. Dave Knight did. He didn't respond much except to stand apart from Delia and let his hands dangle loosely at his sides. Great, I thought, he's just pissed enough to feel like a fight. He probably didn't imbibe that often.

'If you touch that girl it's the end of the road,' I explained.

'Is it?' he said, defiantly.

'Yeah. People are watching. That's what this is all about.'

'People like you, you mean?' he spat. 'Why don't you leave us alone, you nosy bastard? Who do you think is going to believe you, anyway?'

He was clearly greatly taken with Delia. I was going to tell him about the sting, about Knight and the hidden camera, but unfortunately he had crept round to some sort of imagined moral high ground.

'We're two consenting adults,' he blabbered. He was stuttering, but it was anger rather than nerves. 'We have a right to lives of our own. What business is it of yours? It's always people like you who make the trouble, lazy hypocrites who can't be bothered to vote most of the time. It's always people like you who think you have a right to our private lives. Yobs like you who come in and threaten me. Well, you're pathetic. And I won't take this from you!'

He was considerably worked up; a man who I dare say had a few other unresolved personal issues and was several drinks down. If he couldn't screw this girl tonight he was going to throw a tantrum, that much was certain.

'You don't understand,' I told him. 'That girl's a prostitute.'

I would have continued, only he took offence

at this and slipped into stance for a swing. Christ, I tell you, even if a man like that had landed one I'd have collapsed like a pack of cards. I'd taken two bad beatings and my liver had packed up: more friction of any kind would kill me, or so it felt. And if he got me into trouble one of the first policemen I'd see would probably be Dave Knight, and then I'd be dead, because I hadn't even been arsed to turn the camera on. But panic hit me first, and then I noticed I was still carrying this bottled lager in my hand. I think I saw him draw back for a punch, or maybe that's something I've managed to insert after the act, and then he went down. I really tried to avoid the face and go for the top of the head but it wouldn't surprise me at all if he got an inch or so of scar that ran past the hairline.

Delia didn't scream or even whimper. Being a working girl she must have seen her fair share of ugliness; I assume even the upmarket women cannot be safe from exposure to some degree of violence. Her sole response was to press back up against the mirrored wall of the lift as if her reflection were going to let her in.

'Delia,' I said. 'I didn't mean to do that, but I had to stop him. Listen to me: this job isn't what it seems. The woman you spoke to on the phone the other night is a police officer. There's a couple of others, and they're all bent, and they want to blackmail this guy. I didn't know this when I was hired, I found out today. Don't speak to any of them, don't have any more contact with the woman, don't frequent anywhere you think they might be. They're killers. Do you believe me?'

Ping, went the lift, and the doors opened on to the fifth floor.

'My real name isn't Delia,' she said, crying but not making a sound. 'It's Cathy.'

'OK, Cathy. Give me the room key. Now go. Take the stairs.'

As soon as the girl had gone I went through Dixon's pockets and lifted his wallet. It wasn't much of an imposition, not if you bear in mind what I'd just done for him, and that he was a twat. He had over a hundred on him easy, and that was now all the money I had in the world. Then, in what to a lesser man might seem like a fit of recklessness stemming from an unconscious desire to be caught, I went to the hotel room I'd hired and swiped all the miniatures.

On the way back I passed the lift, which was still stuck on the fifth floor, so I pressed the down button and once the doors opened I moved Dixon's leg so it protruded out into the hall. It would stop him surreptitiously beating me to the lobby, where the arrival of a bloodied unconscious body would cause a bit more of a stir than it would in Bedminster Parade. Then I was straight out past reception, my hands spread wide over the bulging pockets of my jacket, trying to stifle the triumphal clinking of stolen spirits in small bottles.

The guy in the top hat held the door open for me.

PART IV

ESCAPE

CHAPTER 1

I t probably goes without saying that there were no fanfares or trumpet blasts. Neither were there any pistol barrels in the small of my back, encroaching sirens or threatening figures stepping out of the shadows. The swing of a cosh did not once slice the air. It wasn't even raining, although there was plenty of water on the ground, and also it was bitterly cold. There was just a man walking briskly to the station for his train.

I did expect it, some kind of violent redress on the part of my employers. I would have put good money on it, but they did not surface. It didn't stop me being afraid that perhaps they might grow tired of waiting, that they might speculatively inspect the hotel, that they might note the absence of all three protagonists and spot my Rover abandoned in the car park. Then it wouldn't take awesome deductive powers to suggest a visit to Temple Meads, not ten minutes away, where their fleeing detective was waiting to defect. These people had been through my flat: they knew I had nothing worth packing.

The ticket windows were closed and the station

was empty. Two minicabs waited at the rank, their drivers nowhere in sight. The station bar, the kiosks and news-stands, all lay dormant behind their metal screens. I have missed my chance, I thought, it has come too late and I will not see another morning. But in the waiting room on platform three there were half a dozen other impotent stragglers, only two of whom looked like long-term residents, and a wall-mounted monitor told me my train had been delayed. If it was to be believed, I had another forty-three minutes.

I took up position down the far end of the platform, where the trains didn't stop, outside the morbid halogen glow of the lights. If they came to the station the waiting room would be the first place they would look. I settled down in the cold stone doorway of some nameless storeroom or workshop and wrapped my coat around me. The lucky dip in my jacket pocket produced a double measure of Bacardi, and I drank on, feeling more than sober. I listened for the fatal footfall, watched for the looming silhouettes of those I had crossed, but none came and there was nothing to do but wait, and drink.

After, I don't know, half an hour or thereabouts, a jaded but human voice announced on the echoing Tannoy that the delay would be extended by another hour. I was mildly astounded that there was still anyone working here at all. He was very apologetic, sincerely so, but I felt my chances shrink further still almost immediately.

I expected to descend into hysterics; instead I opened another miniature and counted out my remaining cigarettes. Perhaps I didn't have the foresight to perceive a danger not yet manifest, or perhaps I was reconciled, save for the muted tremors running periodically through my body. That could be anything, though – cold, drink, pain; you name it.

Even in the hours of early morning, when the Tannoy told of an outright cancellation, I wasn't as frightened as I thought I'd be, even if in the back of my mind I was conjuring up conspiracy theories all the while. The same tired, tinny voice instructed all lost souls to shuffle to the information point, and I followed suit, half expecting it to be a ruse to draw me out.

Replacement cabs was the rumour, spread about by a yellow-eyed man in a well-worn navy ulster, who said he had been here many times before. Nobody else spoke, and then a stooping, blinking man in a white shirt and fluorescent orange waist-coat was suddenly among us.

'It's been derailed outside Bath,' he said, a nervous twitch pulling at the left side of his face. This man has probably been assaulted for shorter delays than this, I thought, watching him count all frustrated travellers with a pointed finger. 'That's two cabs, then. I'll just go and give the stand a ring.'

The yellow-eyed man nodded his approval.

'Are you going to pay for this up front, or will

we be reimbursed?' he asked, his accent some-where around the Midlands.

'Oh, we'll pay the firm on account,' he said, and turned to leave, but thought the better of it. 'I suppose I should see your tickets first.'

'I don't have one,' I told him, 'I was going to buy one on the train.'

'Oh. Right. Well, the ticket booths are closed now.'

'Can you sell me one?'

He took a few steps back for safety's sake before daring to answer.

'No, I'm not a ticket seller. I can't do that.'

It might not have mattered, I supposed, but the others could all fit into one taxi and a fourth passenger would have meant ordering another. I only had a hundred quid on me, and it was all I had in the whole world. With no idea where or when I'd be getting any more I didn't want to blow most of it on a long-distance cab ride, so what, I asked him, were my alternatives?

'The derailed train should be coming through here in another four or five hours, before the next day's timetable begins. You can wait till then,' he said, 'or . . .'

He didn't finish, for he had nothing else to say. It was only covering fire under which he could retreat, out of striking distance, to the safety of a key-coded door. I called out but he merely broke step and began to jog.

It wasn't the end of the world. I'd been at the

station for two whole hours by then, and if anyone was coming to get me that night then surely they would already have done it. All I had to do, it seemed, was stay out of trouble for the next four or five hours. So on platform three I resisted the temptation to join the tramps in the waiting room, basking in the heat of a three-bar electric fire, and stayed outside on my own. They had no pressing reason to keep the peace, if they were still capable of sentient thought in the first place: the middle of the night and the pair of them were upright and mouthing off at the ether, two litres of White Lightning as yet unopened at their feet. I steered clear and found my old doorway.

My policy was justified. Later, I have no idea when, having lost all track of time, I heard the two of them grappling noisily with a uniformed constable. With enemies like mine a night in the cells would have been the end of me. Maybe, I gasped, they had already spread my description over the airwaves, attached to some heinous and fictional crime. It was just a flash, a transitory panic, and it passed in time for me to get up and follow them out from a safe distance. To see them framed in the arched entrance from the dim depths of the station, and watch him kick them all the way down to the road before walking back to his car and calling in for the night, the last old drunk of his shift defeated. Whatever my illusions these days, I can assure you a fondness for the force is no longer among them.

Temple Meads to Frogmore Street station, to cop-house central? Up off into Temple Gate, pull a U-turn into Redcliffe Way, straight over the roundabout at the bottom of Redcliffe Hill and past the lights at Redcliffe Bridge, hugging the perimeter of leafy Queen Square for a ninety-degree turn, nipping into King William Street and then dashing past the Theatre Royal against the one-way traffic on Queen Charlotte, no problem at this time of night, before breaking out into Baldwin Street and cutting straight over St Augustine's Parade to Colston Avenue, taking the first hard left on to Pipe Lane, following Frogmore Street round till the Culver junction on the right, and then another left and you were in the station car park. Another, what, twenty or twenty-five yards on foot and you'd be inside the citadel, staring at the fading blue paintwork on the stairway walls as you plodded upstairs to the station proper. I know this city too well. I know it as a parent knows their child, or should know. It is ingrained in me. I know it all, every lane, street, road, carriageway and bypass. I know every conceivable route there is, except one, and I have just found it, for the first time. The way out took twenty-two years.

I would trace them all later, from memory, in a dimly lit room. It wasn't going to be much of a homecoming. I had big plans at one time but these things never work out the way you imagined. The road to home is paved with good intentions, so to speak. Even old Dylan Thomas had the sense to die an ocean away, face down in a quiet corner somewhere in one of the biggest urban sprawls in the world.

I turned my back on the copper, still barking into his car radio, and sneaked back into the station. I had the entire place to myself now, the lofty steel and crafted sandstone, Brunel's second lasting legacy to the city. He'd given me two choices, old Isambard, one up on the Clifton Bridge and another down here, and it looked like I was taking the latter. It had come as close as it gets. All I had now was a cramped bedsit somewhere and the bottle, and it was enough. Some people never get the chance to buy a ticket back. I had mine, and the rest, whatever it was, the baggage that you couldn't see, would follow, as it always does. But the worst was over.

I remember once, years ago, being sent round to a second-floor flat above a shop on Gloucester Road for a washing machine. The only person there was a fat woman in a headscarf, doubtless an eastern European Muslim of some description, with a bawling baby safely cradled in her meaty arms. Well, she was no problem, although the pair of them never shut up. I was bent over the machine in their kitchen, trying to unhook and unplug the various what-have-yous, because it's not like taking out a television, removing one of those things, and the place went quiet. Not a dicky bird. Previous to this they could probably hear her in Carlisle, so I looked up to witness the miracle and I saw the stairway full of men. The one in front had a tyre iron.

I have never been a brave man, by which I mean I nearly shat myself, and there could have been a dozen or more of these Algerians or Turks or Yugoslavians or whatever. They looked lethally angry, and silent too, the sort of wordless fury that gets you really worried. Maybe the woman had told them I'd insulted her honour, who knows. I saw a knife on the worktop, a blade half a foot long with a pointed tip, and razor sharp. There was no other way out of the room but through these men, who were too many to be counted, and for an instant I was going to do it. I was going to cut open a few people and hope the rest would run. Over a two-hundred-quid washing machine. It crossed my mind as a serious option, as the only option, and that's no word of a lie.

There isn't much to tell you about the fighting, chiefly because I wasn't really doing very much of that, whereas they practically had to queue up. I never knew whether they went at it any harder for seeing my arm reach, hesitate, and then lower itself. It's not the sort of gesture they would have appreciated had they understood, probably quite the opposite. When they found me I was out on the tarmac round the back, hammered into a thin pulp, with the remains of one broken washing machine dumped on my chest.

The point is, I think, that eventually you have

to take the fall. If, for whatever reason, you get involved in any kind of bad business, if you somehow launch yourself on to the wrong side of things, then sooner or later you have to make the choice between taking the knife or taking the fall, and letting it come. All my life I have told myself there was nothing else I could do but carry on regardless, but now I know there was always at least one alternative: maybe the one thing that everybody does last of all, the thing that stops you from doing anything any more, from being. I can see that now. I am no longer like the patient who has to look away from the needle, and I have chosen to take the fall.

I wonder sometimes whether Knight or his minions will try to track me down. It wouldn't be hard, I'm sure, if I was worth the effort, but to be honest I have no intention of giving them the time. There isn't long to go now, if Dr Jenkins was right, which he usually is, and inside I can already feel the years of abuse tightening around my organs like a noose. In the waiting room the big bottle of White Lightning was still there, the collar around its plastic cap unbroken, and I added it to my collection. When the last Llanelli train finally hissed its way into the station unannounced it was still unopened.

The train was as good as empty. In the first carriage I entered there was a young lad in a Neath top fast asleep, with an unfinished slab of Foster's on the seat next to him. I helped myself to a couple of cans, unable to lower myself to opening the tramps' cider, and moved on. It wasn't to last long, that thin veneer of decency. Outside I could see the last stars of evening spluttering out. The train started to lurch, and the station began to slip away.

I had no idea whether I'd done any good, or made any difference at all. Even now I am largely ignorant about the outcome of what happened that night at the Hilton, which is as it should be, if you are no longer going to be involved. I've stopped bothering with the papers, and they'd tell me next to nothing anyway. I have no idea, but maybe things would have been worse without me, if they'd used some other, more willing stooge. I had made my small contribution to the way things ought to be. It was worth a toast, and so I cracked open my can, watching the warehouses now, and industrial estates, sweep slowly by as unreal as stage scenery. I was leaving. The train had begun its long, arrow-like arc into the rest of the world, and I was on it.

The only other traveller I could see was an old man in a trilby, the exact same hat the pensioner who crossed Windmill Hill always held clamped to his head, to stop the early winter wind from snatching it away. When I started working for McKellan I mourned the passing of that era when men could wear hats and get away with it; it would have set the whole thing off, I felt, a tilted trilby. We sat silently, listening to the carriages ticking against the track as the train gathered speed. He knew better than to say a word, and so did I. Soon we would be out as far as Patchway.

And for the first time I thought, or allowed myself to think, of you, my son. A man now, I suppose. Of your mother I thought every day. Didn't I mention it? I mean to say I remembered her, always, until there was nothing in me but the space where she had been, a hole roughly her shape. So it is with all women, I suspect. You were different, though, more like a piece ripped off or torn away. I would be able to face you now, now that I'm the last person you would want to see. Don't worry, I don't think it's likely to happen. We wouldn't recognize each other, and in any case, I have already said all I can.

It's not that I consider myself redeemed, I'm too old for all that rubbish. Who do I have to redeem me? It's just that I'm sorry, and part of me believes that must count for something. It's the only hope I allow myself to harbour. Well, one of two. I hope you grew up fast, son, not too quick, but fast enough to leave something left. Because there are no fresh starts in this life, no clean slates, no new beginnings: don't believe a soul who tells you so. There are only endings. I wondered idly whether the old man of Victoria Park would make it across the hill that afternoon. Something told me I'd never reach that age.

A filament of deep blue broke out on the horizon, and in the lower stretches of the sky I saw the pink tendrils of dawn gently reaching out to wrestle back the night. Then, like a fuse blowing, we were under the Severn, and all was darkness.